"You can let go

Cripes. Travis was holding Rachel with his other arm, tucked against his body and out of harm's way.

"Oh...sorry...ah, I—" He didn't know what to say because he didn't know what he'd been thinking.

A small handful, a perfect fit, her belly hard and warm against him, she belonged in his arms.

It felt natural and good to hold her.

No! No, no, no. He didn't need a woman in his life right now, especially not one laden with burdens he didn't want to bear.

A funny smile curled her lips. "I truly can take care of myself, Travis. I deal with stuff like this most nights."

"I really didn't know I was doing that."

"I know. I could tell."

The feeling of well-being, and the sense of rightness she engendered in him, shook him so badly that he rushed to let her go.

Before he could, the softest of touches flitted across his ribs. Wonder filled him.

The touch had come from Rachel's big belly.

Dear Reader,

Rodeo Father is my very first Harlequin Western Romance and I am thrilled to be a new member of the Western family.

I have a soft spot for cowboys and babies, so Western fits the bill perfectly for me!

In *Rodeo Father*, nomadic loner Travis Read arrives in yet another town, determined to stick around only long enough to make a home for his sister and nephews. He will move along the second they are settled.

He doesn't count on having his heart stolen by the appealing widow who lives across the street, and by her little girl, too. Travis has had enough burdens to last a lifetime, so he doesn't need this attraction to a pregnant woman.

What he doesn't realize is the profound depth of his own loneliness and the desire to set down roots he didn't know existed.

Travis has lived on the outside looking in for too long. When the widow invites him into a world of tenderness and affection he thought existed only for others, he can't resist.

He has always thought the life of a family man, and of fatherhood, was restricted to others and never meant for him.

Rachel McGuire turns out to be the answer to dreams he wouldn't admit he'd been having. Rodeo, Montana, becomes home.

I absolutely loved writing Travis and Rachel's story. I hope you enjoy reading it!

Mary Sullivan

RODEO FATHER

MARY SULLIVAN

HARLEQUIN® WESTERN ROMANCE

Recycling programs
for this product may
not exist in your area.

ISBN-13: 978-0-373-75744-2

Rodeo Father

Copyright © 2017 by Mary Sullivan

Printed in U.S.A.

A city girl born and raised, **Mary Sullivan** found her mother's anecdotes about growing up in rural Canada fascinating. Mary's first career as a darkroom printer fueled her creativity. When traditional darkrooms disappeared with the advent of computers, she learned enough about the machines to use them to fuel her other passion—writing. Once she redirected her energy to creating stories of romance, her mother's tales came back to her and now she devotes her time to writing about rural life. She chooses cowboys and cowgirls for many of her stories. Her Harlequin Superromance books have won awards and earned wonderful reviews. She is now thrilled to write Harlequin Western Romances, too! She loves to hear from readers and can be reached through her website, marysullivanbooks.com.

Books by Mary Sullivan

Harlequin Superromance

No Ordinary Cowboy
A Cowboy's Plan
This Cowboy's Son
Beyond Ordinary
These Ties That Bind
No Ordinary Sheriff
In from the Cold
Home to Laura
Because of Audrey
Always Emily
No Ordinary Home
Safe in Noah's Arms
Cody's Come Home

Visit the Author Profile page
at Harlequin.com for more titles.

To my wonderful agent,
Pamela Hopkins, who continues to have
faith in me book after book after book.
Offering you a profound Thank You.

Chapter One

Travis Read stood on the outskirts of Rodeo, Montana, and stared at the sorriest excuse for a midway he'd ever encountered.

He'd pulled his truck over for a closer look.

Old rides littered the prairie like a county fair graveyard. Rusty signs hung askew.

A hint he should hightail it out of town before he'd even arrived? Maybe, save for one ride. Front and center, a spit-shined carousel stood out from the other decaying machines as though risen fresh from the grave.

Merry-go-rounds weren't usually on Travis's radar, whimsy being a stranger in his life, but he had his nephews to think about now.

He'd bet both his old Stetson and broken-in cowboy boots the boys would be tickled by the carousel. He was.

Gleaming in the meager late-October sunshine, the merry-go-round seemed like a good omen.

No way, Travis.

Grimly, he straightened his spine. He didn't believe in omens, good, bad or otherwise.

"You look like a man who could use a smile."

A feminine voice drifted out of the early-morning mist that shrouded the hushed countryside, carried on the faint breeze like a melody.

A young woman stepped up behind one of the inanimate

ponies on the ride, materializing with a playful smile and a smear of grease across her left cheek.

One fist gripped a wrench and the other a rag, which she used to burnish a gilded saddle on a white pony. The contrast of that wrench and the small hand charmed Travis. No mean feat. He didn't charm easily.

She thought he could use a smile. Dead right.

The woman grinned and his heart stuttered. Good vibes shimmered from her like sunshine reflecting off clear water.

The corners of his mouth, rusty with disuse, twitched.

"Yes, ma'am, I sure could use one of those." No sense denying the truth she'd picked up on. "You don't see many of these around anymore."

She crossed her arms on the elaborate saddle. "Bet you've seen better looking amusement parks."

"Could use some work."

She laughed. "*That's* an understatement if I've ever heard one." As she stared around the downcast place, her expression became subdued.

Her friendliness had lightened up the gray corners of his heart.

"Nothing a little elbow grease won't cure," he ventured, clumsy in his attempt to make her smile again.

She drew herself up and grinned. Aaah. Better.

"Yes," she said. "You're absolutely right."

Unnaturally drawn to this attractive stranger, Travis leaned forward, his body pressing against a wood-slat fence that needed a hammer, a whole lot of nails and a few coats of paint.

"Someone's done a good job on the carousel." By the look of pride on her face, he'd found the culprit. "Looks great."

She looked great. Her smile warmed the chill in his heart.

"What's your name?" she asked.

He doffed his Stetson. His mom might not have taught him much, but she'd stressed the importance of good manners. "Travis Read."

"Rachel McGuire." Her voice rang like birdsong. "Haven't seen you around town. Just passing through?"

She rested her chin on her crossed arms, her glance flickering toward his truck and horse trailer parked on the shoulder.

"Looks like you'll be staying a while?"

He stiffened. He didn't discuss his life with strangers, a habit ingrained years ago.

Yeah, he planned to stay, but only long enough to get his sister and nephews settled in, and then he'd be moving on.

No sense telling that to Rachel, no matter how attractive he found her humor-filled eyes.

It was none of her business.

"Got hired to work for the Webers," was all he was inclined to share.

"On the Double U? You're fortunate. Udall's a good man. Uma mothers everyone for fifty miles around. As long as you're a hard worker, they'll treat you like gold."

If there were a definition in the dictionary for *hard worker* it would be his name. He'd toiled since he was old enough to shovel shit and straw.

Enough about him.

He pointed to a sign dotted brown and green with rust and verdigris, which arched above the entrance to the park: Rodeo, Montana, Fairgrounds and Amusement Park, Home of Our World-Famous Rodeo.

"Heard a rumor the town's planning on resurrecting that rodeo. Next summer?" Maybe he could earn a few extra bucks. He used to be good.

Damned if she didn't perk right up.

"You rodeo?"

"Been known to ride a bull or two."

The aurora borealis he'd once seen in northern Alberta had nothing on this woman's smile.

Rachel brushed a lock of thick hair from her face. He thought the color might be called tawny. It glowed like liquid honey and looked as soft as a calf's ear.

Her smile dazzled him and sent him off-kilter. She had some powerful mojo that had him falling like a load of bricks. Images tempted him, of cozy nights in his new home with a wood fire burning and a thick blanket on the floor beside the hearth, firelight dancing over golden skin, the two of them naked and indulging in the sweetest exercise known to man—

"Care for a ride?" she asked, eyes wide.

A ride? Was his face that transparent? His cheeks heated like coals in a grill.

His shock must have shown because she frowned and tapped the ornamental saddle. "I won't make it go too fast if that's what you're worried about."

Ohhhh, *that* kind of ride.

Well, hell, that was obvious, wasn't it? She was standing on a carousel in a fairground.

Cripes, Travis, get your mind out of the gutter.

Where the heck had that daydream come from? His dreams had been beaten out of him early on in life.

Even so... A ride on a carousel... He yearned, an ache in his chest for a boyhood that had never existed.

Dusty stirred in the trailer. Travis shouldn't leave him so long, but temptation swayed him.

He'd never been on an amusement park ride in his life. They'd never had money as kids. Later, he'd been busy keeping himself and Sammy fed and clothed, body and soul patched together with spit and determination.

With the likelihood of him still being here next summer paper-thin, this could be his one chance for a carousel ride.

Take it, that inner little boy who'd missed all of this in childhood urged.

Why not? How long would it take? Five minutes? He could spare that.

A laugh burst out of him. "You bet! I sure would like a ride, and you can make it go as fast as you want."

As frisky as a young boy, he put a hand on the top rail and hopped over. The structure creaked under his weight.

"You need to shore up that fence."

A waterfall of feminine laughter cascaded over him. "Ya think?" she asked. "Everything in this park needs work. It's a never-ending job."

Travis stepped up onto the carousel.

Up close, Rachel looked even better. His breath backed up in his throat, his world rocked by this one short woman.

She still stood behind the white pony. What he could see of her above its body sure looked fine.

Freckles dotted a pert nose and strong cheekbones. Flecks of gold flashed in eyes lit with an inner glow.

That her hazel eyes and some of the streaks in her hair matched was about the most striking feature he'd ever seen on a woman.

One small freckle dotted her bottom lip.

The tiniest pair of silver cowboy boots hung from stars in her earlobes.

He wondered what the rest of her looked like. With her arms crossed on top of the pony, the too-long sleeves of a plaid flannel jacket covered most of her hands. Her right hand still gripped the wrench.

Inside the collar of her jacket was a prettier shirt collar, Western, pink with white piping and small white flowers embroidered on the tips.

She caught him studying the flowers. "Bitterroot," she said. "Montana's state flower."

A straw cowboy hat with a pink band embroidered with

more bitterroot flowers hung behind her on the center column of the ride.

She flung an arm wide to encompass the characters on the old ride. The pungent scent of fresh paint and turpentine wafted from the structure. "Take your pick. I've been fine-tuning the engine and oiling her parts to put her to bed for the winter. I need to test her. Might as well have a passenger on board while I do."

She smiled again. "Waste of energy otherwise, running her with no one on her. This lovely old lady was made to be enjoyed." In her voice, he heard a world of affection.

"Choose your animal and climb on," she said.

Travis walked around the carousel and rubbed his hand across the backs of the odd animals—odd for an amusement park ride, that was. Along with the usual horses were a pair of bighorn sheep, a bison, a cow, a white-tailed deer and an elk, all wearing ornate saddles. Strangest darned ride he'd ever seen.

He chose a big black bull.

"Predictable," Rachel muttered, tempering it with a humorous tone.

"Sorry to disappoint, ma'am, but I've never seen a bull on a carousel ride before. It's big and sturdy."

In her quick glance down his big body, he saw admiration, but her eyes shifted away too quickly. So was she attracted to him? Or not?

"The bull should hold your weight," was all she said.

He mounted. It did. He held on to a pair of long hard horns.

"Ready when you are," he called back over his shoulder when he heard her walk away behind him.

From somewhere near the center column of the big old thing, she called, "Here you go."

He heard a lever being moved. The ride took a few arthritic strides. Then the engine kicked in and picked up speed.

His breath caught. There was something to be said for taking your first ride as an adult.

"Hang on to your hat, mister. You're going for the ride of your life."

On this old thing? Not likely.

He liked her sense of humor. Together, they could have a lot of fu-u-u-u-n-n—

The carousel picked up more speed than a machine this large and heavy should. Travis gripped the horns. A breeze rushed past his ears, filling them with whispered sighs and longings he'd thought he'd given up on years ago.

"You want music?" she called.

"Yeah!"

The toots and whistles of a calliope filled the air with the old Beatles song "All You Need Is Love."

Stress, responsibility and apprehension fell away, lifting his spirits. When had he ever been free?

Unadulterated joy filled him, the kind kids never question, but that had never had a place in Travis's childhood.

There'd been tangled bits of hope hidden in miserly corners of his world, but there had never been joy.

He let go of the horns and spread his arms wide. The cool wind worked its way through his jacket and shirt, filling him with vitality and refreshing his tired mind. The sun, having finally burned off the morning fog, melted the permafrost of his heart.

His cowboy hat, part of his head for nearly twenty years, flew off.

A huge laugh startled out of him, snatched immediately by the wind and caught by Rachel. He heard her laugh in response.

After a time, the ride slowed and he wiped rivers of tears from his cheeks. He wasn't crying. No. It was just the wind.

He smiled harder than he had in a long, long time.

"That's more like it," Rachel said as she waddled over, satisfaction tinting her tone. "That's the kind of smile I like to see on a man's face."

Whoa. Back up. *Waddled?*

Her pregnant belly stuck out a mile. His dreams of warm winter nights, a fire in the hearth and a willing partner deflated like a weather balloon in a snowstorm.

The woman was about to pop. What was she having? Triplets?

When other people saw pregnant women, they got warm fuzzies. Not Travis.

Pregnant women made him think about being trapped, about expectations and responsibilities. He'd had his fill of those. Still did. Big time.

He had one big responsibility to handle in this town before hitching a ride on the next good breeze and heading back out.

Reluctantly, he dismounted, his dreams slow to die. But die they did. As always.

Oh, Lord, mischief lurked in Rachel's hazel eyes. Damn the woman. She'd known exactly how attracted he'd been to her and how shocked he was now.

"Nice meeting you, Travis. I'm sure we'll see each other around town." She handed him his hat.

He settled it onto his head slowly, tamping it down with a hard tug, the grown man firmly back in place.

"Thank you, ma'am." He might be disappointed in her pregnancy, but she'd given him a gift. His gratitude was sincere. He adjusted his expectations and left the carousel, his stride long and fierce.

He couldn't get away fast enough, driving without a backward glance.

He didn't believe in new beginnings. No matter where he went, he always ended up in the same old place.

Not so for his nephews. Travis wouldn't let that happen to Jason and Colt. Damned if he would let them down. They deserved a good home, and he would create one for them here in Rodeo. They would get more out of childhood than he ever had.

Screw your head on right, Travis. Disappointment never killed a man. Get on with it.

With purpose compelling him forward, he put Rachel out of his mind and drove straight to the Double U, where he pulled up in front of a sprawling ranch house with cedar siding and red shutters framing wide windows.

No one answered the front door when he knocked.

He'd been here once before, the day he'd been hired, put in touch with the Webers by an acquaintance, a cowboy he respected and trusted.

That day, he'd taken a tour of the town and had known immediately it would work for Samantha and the boys.

He'd chosen a house for them, one that had been put on the market just a half hour before he stepped into the real estate office. The down payment had been a result of years of having nothing to spend his paycheck on but himself... and he didn't need much.

A good, solid house. Needed some work, but it had been built well. A safe town. Meant to be.

Travis might not believe in good omens for himself, but he did for his only remaining family.

He ran his new boss, Udall Weber, to ground in the stable.

Udall shook hands with a firm grip. "Good to see you again. You get settled in all right?" A big man with a ruddy complexion, his skin had been ruined by years of hard work in the unforgiving elements.

"Not yet. Got an appointment in an hour to pick up the keys. Meantime, where can I put Dusty?"

"Last stall on the right. First, let's saddle up for a quick tour of the ranch."

"Glad to have one."

"Take the weekend to get yourself organized. Monday will be soon enough to start work. We got fences that need mending before winter."

Travis backed his horse out of the trailer. Dusty, a solid gray gelding he'd owned for a dozen years, had covered a lot of miles with him. His brief visits to get Sammy and the boys out of Vegas and settled in San Francisco seemed like a bad dream here on the stunning Montana prairie.

"Park your trailer behind the barn beside mine." Udall pointed to a spot. "Don't mind if you store it there for the winter till you get your place set up."

"Thanks. Appreciate it." His place never would be *set up*, not for permanently holding cattle.

His clothes were in a bag on the backseat of his pickup truck. His motorcycle rested in the bed. What else did he need?

Sammy's voice rang in his head. *You need a home, Travis. Put roots down somewhere and stay for longer than a year.*

Nope.

"You meet anyone in town yet?" Udall asked, breaking into his thoughts.

A picture of whiskey-colored eyes and tawny hair flashed across his memory. "I stopped at the amusement park outside of town. Met a woman named Rachel."

The corners of Udall's mouth turned down. "Rachel McGuire."

Travis frowned. "You don't like her?"

"I like her fine. Lovely young woman. She's got a rough road ahead, though. Husband's dead and she's pregnant, with another little one already at home."

"Jeez, that's tough."

Wind knocked out of him, Travis had to admit he was

one of the lucky ones. Sure, he had his problems, but that poor woman…what a future she had facing her.

His admiration grew. How she'd kept her good humor boggled his mind. Another kid at home as well as one on the way? Warning bells clanged. No matter how much he admired the woman, he'd be keeping his distance.

"What's with the carousel? It's great, but the rest of the place looks abandoned."

"We got us a committee that's reviving the park. They've set their sights on getting it up and running by next summer."

"Think they can?" Considering what he'd seen today, Travis had his doubts.

"If anyone can, it would be Rachel and her gang."

With a rough laugh, Udall strode away to saddle up, his denim jeans and shirt emphasizing his lean, hard frame.

Travis saddled Dusty, a chore he'd done thousands of times before. This was where he belonged, with horses and ranchers. Running his hand along the horse's neck, he murmured, "You survive the trip okay, boy?"

He rode out with his new boss onto land as pretty as any he'd ever seen. He'd been raised in Arizona, a state with its own brand of stark beauty, but often arid. He liked the colors of Montana.

"Monday morning, we'll get you out trailing," Udall said. "One of the hands spotted a dozen cattle holed up in the gully at the south edge of the property."

Travis followed him out onto the range.

"In his reference letter, Lester Green said you're one of the best he's ever seen at flushing cattle out of tough spots and bringing them home. Said you did real good up in Wyoming last fall."

"Yeah. Lester was a good boss." Travis loved trailing, one of his favorite jobs. "It's late to be finishing up gathering cattle for the winter, isn't it?"

"Yep. Had a couple of the hands out sick. Some kind of flu goin' 'round."

They spotted a sheep caught on a piece of damaged fence on the far side of a field of dormant alfalfa.

"You keep sheep?" Travis asked.

"My neighbor raises them and spins her own yarn."

Together, they got the distressed animal off the fence, but not before it kicked Travis in his ribs.

He hissed.

"That hurt, I bet." Udall said.

Travis rubbed the injury. "Part of the job."

Udall set the animal loose on its own side of the fence. "I'll come back with tools tomorrow and fix this."

"Let me."

Udall shot him a surprised look. "You sure? You only just got here."

"I'm sure. Just spent too many days on the road. I'm itchy to get out on the land."

Udall smiled approvingly. They mounted and rode on.

So darned glad to be back in the country, Travis breathed deeply of fresh air purer than anything he'd ever found in any city.

His worries fell away, leaving only the wind in his ears, the sun on the prairie and the warmth of the animal beneath him.

Chapter Two

Rachel McGuire rested her head against the inanimate pony's unforgiving neck, unsure whether to laugh or have a good, hard cry.

What on earth had just happened to her poor battered heart?

The second she'd laid eyes on the new arrival, Travis Read, she'd been attracted to him.

What kind of man could melt her hardened heart with just a look from blazing blue eyes, the rustiest of smiles and so few words? And not just her heart, but also her pregnant body, waking it from a long slumber.

Could the timing possibly be worse?

What kind of poor, dumb fool was she for finding a man so attractive when she was more than seven months pregnant, and as big as that horse she'd heard shuffling in his trailer?

She'd wanted to flirt. But why would he ever be interested in her?

That smile? When he'd ridden the carousel? Oh, sweet heavenly pumpkins, pure and utter joy.

She'd given him a simple ride on a carousel, and he'd smiled at her as though she'd hung the moon.

And all of that lovely warmth and admiration she'd basked in had come to a crashing halt when he'd seen her belly.

Of course she understood why. Totally got it.

But wouldn't it be nice to be carefree and available to flirt with a man who'd found her attractive?

Suck it up, Rachel. This is the life you chose. Live it.

Rachel laughed at her lapse in common sense. "You so need to get over yourself, Rach."

She put the finishing touches on the carousel, preparing it for the coming winter. An hour later, she tucked away her tools, along with her unreasonable attraction to the new man.

She drove into town and stopped at the used-clothing shop.

Her wardrobe was pretty slim pickings at the moment.

She found a glittery maternity top she could wear to work. If she took off the sequins and rearranged the beading, she could remake the top into her own style. Embroidery, sewing and knitting calmed her. That she could take a five-dollar top and make it personal filled her with pride.

At the market, she shopped for next week's groceries. In the produce section, she found marked-down overripe bananas that would make an excellent bread.

She picked up fruits and vegetables on special and root vegetables in season.

A huge bag of lentils was on sale. Good source of protein. She bypassed the expensive sugary cereals and instant oatmeal to pick up a bag of rolled oats. By the time she finished, she had an economical, nourishing menu planned for the weekend and coming week for herself and her daughter.

Maybe I should get a small steak to share with Tori. Her mother was always on her case about eating meat for the baby, and Tori was a growing girl who needed protein.

She perused the packages, but the prices worried her. She picked up one minuscule steak, shuffling along the counter to see if there was a better deal, until she ran smack dab into a hard body.

She looked up.

Travis Read. Here. In the grocery store.

Good grief. Was her heart going to do somersaults every time she met him? Or bumped into him? Literally.

He grasped one of her upper arms to steady her, his big palm warm even through Davey's thick old jacket.

"I'm sorry!" Her heart thumped at just the sight of him let alone the touch of those long fingers. "I wasn't watching where I was going."

Rachel's skin seemed to constrict until it was a size too small for her body.

"No problem," he said. "No harm done."

The thick honey of his deep voice flowed along her nerves. Her pulse skittered a foolish teenage girl's dance in her mature woman's body.

Travis had a great mouth, finely shaped with a firm outline. How would his lips feel on hers? Would his kiss be more refined than Davey's had been? Her husband's kisses had been long on enthusiasm and short on finesse. She had a feeling Travis loved on a whole different level.

Get a grip, Rach.

"You okay?" Travis asked. He glanced down.

Too late, she remembered she'd opened her jacket when she'd entered the store. Her shirt wasn't maternity and didn't fit properly. Only the top three buttons were done up, and the bottom of the shirt splayed over her big belly.

Her nicer maternity jeans were hung up at home, waiting for her to put them on for work.

The pants she had on now, a pair she'd bought secondhand, were already worn out from her first pregnancy. The belly panel was stretched to the max, showing white flecks where the elastic had broken.

Good grief.

The silence went on too long. "You made it to the Double U?"

"Yeah. Made it there just fine."

A dark shadow painted his strong jawline. He smelled of citrus. His body generated heat.

She stepped away.

Come down to earth, she scolded herself.

She dropped the one barely there steak she'd picked up onto her discounted vegetables and lentils. His basket held seven steaks. Seven!

Her economic situation had never embarrassed her in the past. Frustrated her? Oh, yeah. But caused her shame? No. It had merely been a fact of her life. It disconcerted her now, though.

Neither of them had said anything for a while. Their silence fell into truly awkward, uncomfortable territory.

"Don't forget to add some vegetables," she blurted.

Cripes, small talk had never stressed her out before. She could usually talk the paint off a barn door, yet here she stood with her mouth gone as dry as a popcorn fart.

Travis sidled away from her, hefting the basket with a rueful kick up of one side of his mouth. "Yeah, guess I'll grab a few potatoes."

"And greens." *Brilliant conversation, Rach.*

He grimaced. "Maybe."

She managed a reasonable facsimile of a grin. "Which means you won't."

His sweet fraction of a shy smile made a brief appearance.

He doffed his hat and left. "See you 'round town, Rachel."

She watched him stride away.

The phrase *salt of the earth* came to mind. Travis Read would fit in well in Rodeo, maybe better than she did. After all, she wasn't much of a cowgirl. She didn't ride horses, and she didn't live on a ranch.

She loved Montana, though, and loved her town with all of her heart. Rachel adored its basic, varied, salt-of-the-earth residents. She was working her fingers to the bone on next summer's fair to keep the town alive and make it prosperous again.

Tamping down her wayward daydreams, she paid for her purchases.

At home, she poured a glass of OJ, taking it and an oatmeal muffin outside to soak up the rays of what might be one of the last good days of autumn.

She sat on the porch step—*porch* being a generous term for the slice of tilting wood and two steps hammered together under the front door of her mom's trailer.

Sunlight flooding the valley reflected off the tarnished white wood siding of the Victorian across the road.

Rachel sighed. She missed Abigail Montgomery, her elderly friend. Her death, days after Davey's, had been devastating. Worst time of her life.

She'd lost too much six months ago. Thoughts of her big, irrepressible Davey... Whew! Those could still bring her to her knees.

She wrapped her arms around herself and rocked. She missed him every night.

She'd already cried a river for him, and for Abigail, but she had a life to live and children to raise. She needed her good spirits to help shoulder her burdens.

Veering away from her grief before it brought on tears, she concentrated on the Victorian.

Her every-second-of-the-day dream about owning that house perked her up, rerouting her thoughts away from devastating memories.

To everyone else in Rodeo, the aging home looked like a run-down romantic anomaly in the Western landscape, but to Rachel it was perfect.

But then, romantic notions and daydreams had always been her downfall, hadn't they?

Davey had never known about this particular dream. She'd wanted to surprise him with a fait accompli. *Look, honey, I bought us a house.*

Any day now it would be hers. She hadn't heard even a whisper about whether Abigail's British relatives were going to put it up for sale, but why wouldn't they?

It was useless to them.

She'd scrimped and saved until she had just shy of five thousand dollars in change and small bills hidden in her closet.

Dumb spot to keep her money, but she and Davey had had a joint bank account. Had he known about this money, he would have siphoned off every spare cent for his motorcycle passion…or for treating his friends to beer every Friday night…or for chewing through money like it was cereal.

Davey had had those great big hands that could love her with enthusiasm, but they were a pair of sieves where money was concerned.

She should roll the change and count the money soon and get it into the bank. Later. Right now she needed these moments of rest.

The pretty trills of a horned lark on Abigail's land floated across to her on the late-October breeze.

No one else in town would want that house.

There was no way there would be a speck of competition. It needed work.

It would be hers. It could have been hers a lot sooner had she married someone more practical.

The heart has a mind of its own, Rach, and you just have to follow it.

I sure did, didn't I?

Yes. She sure had, right back into the financial insecurity she'd grown up with.

She let out a sigh full of hot air and yearning.

The distant hum of an engine—a motorcycle—cut through her daydreaming. Her unreasonable heart lurched with thoughts of her late husband.

A big Harley shot down the old road toward her.

It wasn't Davey, of course. Never again would her husband ride home with a shit-eating grin that would light up any cloudy day.

She scrubbed her hands over her arms and shivered despite the sunshine. Oh, Davey.

The bike came close, closer, and slowed down enough to initiate the turn into Abigail's driveway. Who was it?

The noise disturbed the lark. Routed, he surged from his hiding spot, his distinctive yellow-and-black face catching the eye of a white cat crouching in the grasses along the side of the road. *Ghost.* Abigail's cat shot out toward the songbird, right into the bike's path. *No!*

Rachel stumbled to her feet. "Get back," she yelled.

The biker swerved to avoid the cat, Ghost ran back into the tall grasses and the bike tipped over. The machine flew across the road, screeching and shooting sparks, leaving the rider bouncing and rolling along the shoulder in a plume of dust.

In the ensuing silence, dirt and stones fell on his still body.

Rachel froze. Unwelcome memories of that awful day and the police officer at her door surged through her. *He's gone, ma'am, in a head-on collision with a tree. I'm sorry.*

Resurrected shock held her immobile.

The man lay unmoving.

Rachel stared. *Please, not another death. Abigail. Davey. No.*

A groan from across the small highway galvanized her.

Rachel ran over, the only sound her pounding pulse.

He still hadn't moved. *Oh, dear Lord, please don't die.*

Kneeling beside him, she checked his body for signs of injury. Hard to tell through the leather. She touched his shoulders, arms and legs, feeling for broken bones. Under layers of solid muscle everything *seemed* fine, but what about internal injuries? She didn't know how to check. With a wail of frustration, she tore into herself for never having taken first-aid classes.

One arm moved, raising the visor of his helmet.

Her frantic glance took in his face. He was conscious. Deep-set blue eyes watched her steadily, silently.

He reached up to remove his helmet. She stopped him with a hand on his wrist, feeling a strong pulse, thank God. "Should you do that? Is your head injured?"

Her voice shook. So did her hands.

"I'm good." He took off his helmet, and she gasped.

Travis?

Of all people—What—? How—?

"Are you okay?" Her voice emerged reed thin.

He didn't respond, just stared into her eyes, then touched her bottom lip with a glove-clad finger.

"Only one," he murmured.

Huh?

His eyes met hers again, mesmerizing. She could fall into that blue gaze for hours. The moment stretched out. A smile, sweet and broad, curved the corners of his mouth.

Oh my-y-y. What did Travis use for toothpaste? Moonbeams?

He sat up slowly, his body coming close enough for her to feel his heat even through his leathers. She sat back on her heels.

She should tell him to be careful, to check for injuries, but couldn't find her voice.

His hand brushed a strand of hair from her forehead, the

leather soft against her skin. Grasping the tips of his glove with his straight white teeth, he tugged it off, then did the same with the other. Still mesmerized, Rachel stared, swallowed and stared some more.

Again he reached for her hair and ran his fingers through it, massaging her scalp. Rachel almost purred like a cat.

"Soft," he said. "Calf's ear." He wasn't making sense, but Rachel was too captivated to question him while he touched her with such gentle grace. Her traitorous desire overrode her common sense.

She moaned low in her throat.

He moved his hand to the back of her neck, urging her close to his chest. As pliable as a rag doll, she allowed it. His lips touched hers with velvety moisture and a faint exhalation of coffee-scented breath.

She hadn't touched a man since Davey. Davey. Her late husband. Her eager, playful lover.

Pull back, Rach. Don't allow this. Davey is only six months gone. You should—

He deepened the kiss. Taking his time, he caressed her tongue with his. His skill. Oh, his earnest, deep skill. Yes, to his awesome finesse. She'd known it would be like this. Heavenly bliss.

Rapture. Joy.

Need simmered inside her. In the months since Davey's death, what she had needed most was his touch, his soothing physical support, one last endless night of blazing lovemaking.

A woman should be allowed to say goodbye to her husband. Rachel's anger wrestled with her guilt and desire.

Fireworks blazed. Buried dreams came to life. This man's touch, his mouth, soothed away aching, aching grief.

Rachel sighed and lost herself in his kiss, exploring his mouth with her ardent tongue.

She'd never kissed, had never been kissed, so slowly and intently. Her mind went blank and her body limp.

Elizabeth announced her presence with a hard kick to Rachel's belly.

She pulled back. "Ouch." She'd been kneeling too long.

"Ouch?" Travis's voice sounded lost in a sensual fog, echoing how she felt.

"The baby kicked me. I need to stand up."

"Baby?" Coming out of his daze, his eyes widened. Horror spread across his features. "Sorry! God, I'm sorry. I shouldn't have done that."

"You've had a shock," she managed to bite out, while she really wanted to blurt, *Don't be sorry. I've never been kissed like that in my life. I needed it. After all of the turmoil, and the crazy worries about the future, I needed something for me. Purely, selfishly, for just me.*

But that was a daydream that required a hasty burial. *Just me* was not possible these days.

She eased away from him and rubbed her belly to soothe Beth.

"Are you okay?" she asked, striving to pretend she hadn't been rocked by a stranger's kiss, that this was nothing out of the ordinary.

"Yeah." He nodded with a perplexed frown.

Did he understand any better than she what had just happened?

"Should I call an ambulance?"

"No ambulance. No hospital. I'm good."

The cowboy she'd met a short while ago was gone, replaced by a motorcycle rider. "No head injury? You were out cold."

"Naw. Not out cold, just winded."

"But you didn't move when I was checking you for injuries."

"No, I didn't." His jaw hardened, so briefly she barely caught it. She didn't have a clue what was going on.

He stood and winced. "This head's pretty hard. I've survived worse. Gonna be bruised tomorrow, though."

Rachel struggled to get to her feet. Travis rushed to help her. "You shouldn't be kneeling in your condition."

In her condition. For a brief moment, she hadn't been a pregnant woman, but a desirable one. He'd looked past her circumstances to *her*.

She stared at him. "Are you serious, Travis? I thought you were unconscious. I needed to check you. You could have been badly hurt."

"I appreciate your concern," he said, his hands strong beneath her elbows, lifting her as though she weighed no more than a sack of potatoes. "I'll be stiff the next few days, but that's all." He made sure she was steady on her feet, took her hands in his and squeezed before he released her, his rough calluses a jolting return to reality.

She needed reality, needed to get her head back onto her shoulders. So, he hadn't been knocked out, but maybe he'd been in shock. How else to account for that kiss? He hadn't known he was kissing *her*. Maybe he'd thought she was an old girlfriend. Or a current one? After all, she was nothing to him.

His leather jacket had a tear along one arm. Travis could have been killed.

On a dime, those awful memories raced through her again. Davey, Davey, Davey.

Her blood arced and swooped through her arteries. Her pulse skittered worse than on a caffeine high. "You sure you don't have internal injuries?"

"No injuries. Everything feels fine. Good thing I slowed down to take the turn."

Rachel reached down to swipe dirt and gravel from her

knees. A fine tremor ran through her. Anger overtook the fright he'd given her.

She couldn't fend off images, thousands of Davey carefree and laughing, and that one horrifying imaginary picture of him broken by the side of the road thanks to his damned obsession with motorcycles. Because of them, he was gone for good, and her children were fatherless. What was it with men and their stupid, dangerous toys? *Unfair, Rachel. A motorcycle is just a tool.* Davey's reckless speed had been the real problem.

Common sense held no sway, only anger. "Maybe you should stop riding motorcycles. They're dangerous."

At her sharp tone, he shot her a hard look. "Not if you know what you're doing. Was that your cat that ran out in front of me?"

"No, it was Abigail's."

"Who's Abigail?"

Rachel pointed to the aging Victorian. "That was her house."

"Right," he said. "I thought the owner died months ago. Who owns the cat now?"

"Ghost turned feral after her death." Rachel drew a breath to steady her quavering voice. This man's decisions were no concern of hers. Who was she to judge what he did with his life? She modulated her tone. "She won't come near anyone. I'm worried about her."

"She's gonna get herself killed."

"That's what I'm afraid of."

He strode to his bike and lifted it onto its tires, the machine as light as a bicycle in his capable hands. He was strong, but then again, she already knew that.

Where Davey had been tall and lean, Travis was maybe five-eleven and heavily muscled.

He turned the bike toward the house.

Those memories of Davey still haunting her, she couldn't help but ask again, "Are you sure you're all right?"

His soft smile eased her anger, a bit. "Yeah, I'm good. Honest. How about you? You good?"

"I'm fine."

He touched a couple of fingers to his forehead in a casual salute—no wedding band, not that she was looking—and then limped up the driveway toward the Victorian.

"Wait!"

He turned back.

"Why were you riding a bike? Where's your truck?"

"Left it in the garage for a checkup. It's been running rough, and I want it ready for winter."

"Where's your horse and trailer?"

"Udall's letting me leave them on his ranch till I'm set up here."

Here? At Abigail's?

"Why are you going to Abigail's house? Won't you be bunking in the worker's quarters on the Double U?"

"Nope. I'll be living here." He parked his bike at the side of the driveway. She followed him.

Living here. In Abigail's house, which she hadn't even heard had been rented. Travis would be living across the road from her, where she would have to see him every day and remind herself that no amount of makeup or dresses could change what she was…an ungainly woman who was a month and a half away from giving birth. No amount of dolling up would make her as attractive to him as he was to her.

But he'd kissed her.

He'd been stunned, dazed, that was all. She would probably never know who he'd really been kissing while he'd put his lips to hers so sweetly.

"No one told me the house had been rented."

"Rented? No, ma'am. I bought the place." He mounted the stairs to the veranda.

Bought—? Her house had been *sold*? When had it been listed, and why hadn't she heard about it? This was a small town. Everybody's business was an open book, for God's sake, and not one person had thought to tell her the house she craved had been sold?

What do you expect, Rach? You kept that dream close to your chest, didn't you?

True, she had. She hadn't wanted people, not even Davey, to think poor Rachel McGuire was crazy enough to believe she could actually find a way to buy a house.

Maybe she hadn't heard him properly.

She chased after him, stood at the bottom of the stairs and stared up at him.

"You're joking, right?"

He frowned down at her from the top of the steps. "Why would I joke?"

"You're not supposed to be living here. No one's supposed to buy this house." She sounded like a lunatic. She didn't care.

Her house, the only thing she wanted more in life than her children's health and happiness, had been sold.

The air became thin.

She panted. Stars danced in front of her eyes. Her vision narrowed. A moment later, she found herself sitting on the bottom step with a hand on her back urging her head between her knees. Hard to do with a nearly full-grown baby in the way. The cowboy squatted in front of her and chafed the backs of her hands.

"Are you all right?"

She straightened, still struggling for air, but not so dizzy.

"Are you hungry or something? You fainted. Good thing I caught you."

She'd fainted and he'd caught her? The man moved fast. "Wait a minute. Back up."

When Travis started to pull away from her, she grasped his hands, craving his solid comfort as her daydreams slid into nightmare. He squatted on his haunches and watched her with a steady regard.

"I didn't mean get away from me," she said. "I meant, back up in the conversation. Please tell me I misunderstood. You did *not* buy this house."

"I bought the house."

"No." It came out a croak, with tears clogging her throat. This house was supposed to be hers.

He watched her with pity. Great.

As if it wasn't bad enough that she was Cindy Hardy's daughter and a widowed, single mother with a bun in her oversize oven and a three-year-old daughter with no father, and that they lived in Cindy's tin can, but now she had also lost the chance to own the only house in the county she could have ever hoped to afford...and the only one she'd ever dreamed of owning.

Sure, her itty-bitty down payment would buy a small trailer, but after the childhood she'd had, the thought made her sick. She wanted more for her children. She wanted a real home.

The man who had bought her house watched her as if he was afraid she would faint again.

A terrible rage arose in her.

She didn't want pity. She wanted a knock-down, drag-out fight, to pound something hard and not stop for a good month.

Bursting with the unfairness, she pushed against the cowboy squatting in front of her. Travis fell onto his butt in the dirt.

"Hey!"

Rachel had never touched another person with violence in her life.

She stood. Her belly might make a swift exit impossible, but she couldn't stay here.

He jumped to his feet and grasped her upper arms to stop her. "Why'd you do that? I've done nothing to you."

She kept her mouth shut because, if she didn't, she would start to scream and never stop.

His big hands still gripped her arms. She hated him. She didn't want him to stop touching her.

She put her hands against his chest to push him away, but her outrage deflated. If she could fall into the earth and disappear, she would. He was right. *He* had done nothing to her. Life had. As hard as she fought, she couldn't get ahead.

Stuff happened.

She was tired of stuff happening.

She would just have to work harder. And harder. And harder. God, she was tired.

"I'm sorry," she whispered, her palms soothed by the solid beat of his heart beneath his worn denim shirt.

Despite his confusion, despite how she had just treated him, he watched her with concern. Travis was kind and good, and she was behaving like a child.

"I truly am sorry."

"It's okay. I can see you're upset."

She started down the driveway to go home, or what passed for a home.

"You're shaky," he called. "You need some help getting across the road?"

Cripes. The day had started so well. For a short while, he'd found her super-duper attractive. Now, he was treating her like an invalid.

"I can manage by myself," she answered with a touch of irritation.

She managed to make it inside the front door before the first tears fell.

After five minutes of the worst pity party she'd thrown for herself since Davey's death, she rinsed her face and called her friend Nadine.

Rachel brought her up to speed on everything that had just happened.

"I'm angry, Nadine. Mad to the soles of my shoes. Life has to start turning around for me sometime soon."

Nadine said, "I hear you, sweetie. You've had a rough go of it. How can I help?"

Nadine wrote for the local newspaper. She was handy with research and a computer.

A need for…something…burned inside Rachel. Vengeance, maybe? Or perhaps just to learn that Travis was *not* the perfect man he appeared to be? That he was flawed and unworthy of her attraction? That he didn't deserve her house? It would be so much easier to think of him as her enemy if she didn't like him so much.

"Find out about him," she ordered Nadine. "You're a great reporter. You do research for your articles. Find out who Travis Read really is and then let me know."

"Will do, honey. I'll get back to you soon."

Rachel wished Tori were home right now. She would give her daughter the biggest hug, but every Friday morning, Cindy and Tori had a standing date for a few hours of shopping and then lunch at the mall.

Cindy worked at the hair salon in town and had disposable income. Cindy cared more for clothes and perfect nails than she did about improving her living situation.

Every week, she gave Tori the treats that Rachel could not afford and, every week, Rachel rose above her own regret and envy to be happy for Tori.

The new mall out on the highway twenty miles away

was a monstrosity into which Rachel refused to set one foot. She liked the shops on Main Street, thank you very much.

Her mom loved the mall, but then, she had no sense of loyalty to her town at all.

Rachel missed Victoria. They'd only been gone a few hours, but Rachel needed her daughter something fierce.

Tori was goodness and light and the antidote to every disappointment life had visited upon Rachel.

She took her straw cowboy hat from the hook beside the door. She'd embroidered the bitterroot flowers on the band herself, as well as the ones on the secondhand shirt she wore. She set it on her head defiantly, then sat on the porch step to wait for her daughter to come home. She shouldn't be wearing straw at this time of year, at the end of October for Pete's sake, but Davey had given it to her after their first date. 'Nuff said.

Chapter Three

What the *hell* had that kiss been about? Travis took himself to task about as hard as he ever had in his life.

What had he been thinking? He knew only that Rachel had run across the road and had touched him with hands more caring than any he'd ever known. Her concern for him, a man about whom no one cared or gave a second thought, was a powerful attraction.

Women usually wanted stuff *from* him, as opposed to worrying about him.

After a childhood as bereft of affection as a snowball in hell, tenderness took him by surprise.

He'd been winded and shocked at losing control of his bike, flat on his back cursing himself for a fool, and then there she was like an angel, leaning over him with thoughtful concern and fear for his well-being.

His parents hadn't cared. His sister would have, but he'd spent too many years taking care of her and their pattern was set in stone. He was the caretaker, not she.

Travis watched the woman waddle back to the sad-looking trailer across the road, stubborn defiance stiffening her spine.

She asked for nothing and offered so much. Too much.

Have a care, Travis. You don't even know the woman and already you're kissing *her?*

He'd never done anything like it in his life. He'd had

plenty of one-night stands, but not with women with pregnant bellies and a whole barn load of responsibility.

Lying in the road with his protective shields down, this morning's attraction had flared.

Her hair turned out to be every bit as soft as a calf's ear. And she'd tasted as sweet as he'd imagined.

But what good was attraction when he could do nothing with it? She was pregnant. He had a glut of duties to fill in the coming months. He didn't need more.

He had his own life to live.

Case closed, Travis. End of story, got it?

He needed to back away from Rachel and *stay* away.

He unhooked his saddlebags from his bike and carried them into his house. *His* house.

Travis Read. Homeowner. He couldn't wrap his head around it.

Home. Lord, how did a man learn how to make a home when he'd never known a single good one in his whole life?

The challenge scared the hell out of him.

The empty rooms waited like hungry sponges to soak up the noise and chaos Jason and Colt would surely create.

Was he doing the right thing in uprooting them and bringing them here? He had only his gut to rely on, and it was shouting a resounding *yes*.

In the old-fashioned kitchen, he unpacked his groceries and put them into the ancient fridge.

Upstairs, he chose the largest bedroom for himself and the new king-size bed he'd ordered. He'd slept in bunkhouses all his adult life. Now he owned a bed.

Soon it would be Samantha's, and he'd be back in another bunkhouse somewhere.

His bags hit the floor with a solid clunk.

Walking back downstairs, he stared around. By the time Sammy and her boys arrived, he needed to turn this house into a home.

He had plenty of work ahead of him, in cleaning up the

place and renovating. Floors needed sanding and walls painting.

He had no template to guide him. He would start with whatever needed fixing and then take inspiration from the many ranch wives who'd made homes and fed him and his fellow cowboys on too many ranches to count.

There was nothing inside him to draw on.

He had plenty of longing, but zero know-how.

Moving on was all he knew, and bunking with a dozen other men was his way of life.

Travis Read. Homeowner. A home meant obligation and duty, a millstone around a man's neck…and he was damned tired of those.

RACHEL SAT ON the porch and watched her mother pull into the driveway and park her decked-out pickup truck beside Rachel's old junker.

Cindy Hardy had no understanding of the notion *less is more.*

She had bought every chrome feature the local dealership could get its hands on.

Thank God Rachel had been able to talk her out of a lift kit.

Cindy mistakenly assumed that men drooled over her, when all they really wanted was her truck.

Too many of the men in town had known Cindy, as in *known* known, to want to have anything to do with her romantically.

To the people of Rodeo, Montana, Cindy had always been and would always be the girl from the trailer park— even if there was no park, only a trailer.

The second Cindy got Tori unbuckled, Rachel's daughter jumped out of the truck, came running toward her mom and threw herself into her arms, squealing, "Mommy, Mommy."

Rachel broke into a huge smile and hugged her little

three-year-old bundle of joy. Cindy unloaded the bags. Rachel oohed and aahed over her daughter's new purchases. Cindy had bought her a lot of fun stuff. Thank goodness it wasn't all toys, but also new clothes. Another week of Cindy's wages down the tubes.

Rachel should tell her to stop, but without Cindy buying Tori's clothes, the child would have little to wear. Besides, how could she tell Tori's only grandmother to stop spoiling her?

Nope. She didn't have it in her heart to ruin Cindy's fun, even if Cindy never had understood that it would have been better to have saved at least some of her money to improve her life's situation than to wait for some man to come along and save her.

Rachel would never, not in a million years, depend on a man again where her finances were concerned. She planned to scrimp and save and work until her knuckles hurt, and then get her children into a stable, secure home life.

Tori chattered away, reminding her of what was at stake.

Davey's parents had both died when he was in high school. Ironic that it had been a car crash.

Cindy was Tori's only other relative apart from Rachel.

Maybe one day a week of being spoiled wasn't so bad.

A sound from the road caught their attention. A truck turned into Abigail's—correction, Travis's—driveway.

Rachel brushed her fingers through Tori's soft blond curls. Mother Nature had fashioned her daughter's hair out of strands of pure sunlight.

She and Tori watched the activity across the road, Rodeo's version of reality TV.

"That's a big chruck, Mommy."

"Truck," Rachel corrected automatically. "It sure is, Tori-ori-o."

With a pang of deep-seated regret, Rachel thought, *My house belongs to someone else now.*

"What's going on over there?" Cindy asked.

Cindy Hardy wore full makeup, and styled and sprayed hair. She'd tucked a sparkly, faux-Western shirt into her favorite jeans, which in turn were tucked into polished gray snakeskin cowboy boots, boots that had never seen the inside of a barn. A big rodeo belt buckle, a gift from a former lover, accentuated a still-trim waist.

Rachel suspected the guy had probably had a bunch of buckles made up expressly to give to women like Cindy. No rodeo rider worth his salt would give his own buckle away.

"It sold, but we didn't hear about it," Rachel said, not bothering to update her mother on details. The thought of introducing her to Travis made Rachel antsy in a way she didn't want to look at too closely.

Cindy was still young and attractive, even if her style wasn't something that appealed to Rachel.

Two men got out of the truck. "Wonder if the new owner will paint," Rachel murmured. "It needs to be freshened up."

Cindy's husky laugh mocked her. "It needs a heck of a lot more than a coat of paint."

Resentment shot through Rachel. "I would have been happy to have done the work to fix it up." A fixer-upper was the only kind of house she could ever hope to buy.

A commotion across the road snagged her attention, as the two burly men opened the rear doors of the truck.

Travis didn't own much. The truck was less than half full. The men unloaded a large dresser and carried it into the house.

Tori marched her fingers up Rachel's leg, singing "The Itsy Bitsy Spider."

Rachel glanced down at her three-year-old daughter,

gazing into eyes so blue they rivaled the cloudless sky, into Davey's eyes, the first thing that had attracted Rachel to him. His brilliant, laughter-filled eyes.

She was struggling to replace his laughter in their lives.

The pair of movers came back for a big leather sofa. "Too masculine. That house needs comfortable, cozy sofas and armchairs. Shabby chic. Chintz."

"Chins," Tori whispered.

The furniture looked brand-new.

Travis came outside, all traces of leather gone. The cowboy she'd met this morning stood on the front porch.

He leaned against a veranda post, a rugged movie star in worn jeans, a snug white T-shirt, denim jacket, well-used cowboy boots and a black Stetson.

He should have looked out of place on Abigail's old-fashioned veranda. He didn't. He looked…perfect.

Cindy whistled. "Good-looking man. *He* bought that house? Wow. Who is he?"

Rachel didn't fill her in. She had never, not once in her life, competed with her mom where men were concerned, but she felt a rivalry now with a raging fire.

"What does he need a whole house for?"

Good question. "I don't know, Cindy."

Rachel had had time to cool down. Contrary to what she'd thought earlier, Travis was not her enemy. He was only a man who'd somehow managed to do better in life than she had.

His glance swept the countryside, Cindy's house, Rachel and Tori…and Cindy.

What good looks Rachel lacked, Cindy had in spades. Tori had inherited her blond curls from her grandmother, along with her charming dimples. Somehow those had bypassed Rachel.

All Rachel had were strong features and freckles, courtesy of a father she'd never met.

"I'm going over to meet him." Cindy squeezed past Rachel and Victoria and stepped down from the porch.

"No!" Rachel didn't want her mother embarrassing her. "Mom, please. Don't—"

"Don't what?"

"Don't flirt with him like you do with every man I meet."

Cindy wouldn't just be welcoming Travis to the neighborhood. She would ramp it up to see what she could get out of the man.

"He's the best-looking man we've had around here in ages. If you think I'm going to pass him up, you're nuts." Cindy rubbed her hands on her thighs, the gesture telling. "I'm still young. I can flirt with any man I want. It's none of your business."

Cindy was pretty enough to turn any man's head, but she'd been plagued with a neediness that routinely drove her into the arms of the wrong kind of man.

Relentless, she was forever on the lookout for her next conquest.

Her sights had just zeroed in on the one across the way.

"Please, Cindy, no. You want to get your hooks into him." Rachel knew Cindy's needs inside and out. The vulnerability in the depths of her eyes was exactly the thing that had gotten her into trouble when she was only fifteen, hitching her pony to a good-looking drifter's wagon and then getting pregnant. Whoever the guy was, he'd been long gone by the time Rachel had been born.

Rachel was twenty-eight and her mother only forty-three. Rachel guessed Travis to be in his mid- to late thirties. Cindy could conceivably flirt with him, but what a load of trouble it could bring.

"Mom, he's not a drifter. He's our new neighbor. He bought the house, for Pete's sake."

"So?"

"So…" Rachel said with forced patience. "This could go wrong in so many ways."

"Everything will be fine. I'm only going over to talk to him." In Cindy's voice, Rachel heard the hints of desperation that had been growing stronger since Cindy had turned forty.

"And when the relationship goes sour, as it always does?" Rachel's displeasure bubbled over. She'd seen this movie too many times and hated the ending. "How good a neighbor will he be then? How good will *you* be?"

Cindy shrugged. "Maybe this time it will work out." She started to mosey down the driveway, but turned back. "You could always move into a place of your own, and then you wouldn't have to watch me talk to men." She walked across the road.

Mom was right. This was her mother's home, not hers. Cindy could flirt with whomever she wanted. "Come on, sugar pie, let's go inside," Rachel said, urging Tori ahead of her, unwilling to witness Cindy's performance.

Inside the house, she strode to the kitchen and settled Tori into a chair.

In the bedroom, Rachel chose one of her few maternity shirts and put it on with her good maternity jeans.

She returned to the kitchen where she put the finishing touches to the dinner she'd made to take to work with her, every action staccato and peevish.

She had no claim on the new stranger. Cindy could do whatever she wanted with him.

She packed a quinoa salad and a pint of milk, dropping them into her bag too hard.

Forcing herself to calm down, she took Tori's tiny face between her hands. Rachel kissed her forehead and her nose. "I love you, sweetie. Come sit on the porch and wave goodbye."

She picked up her purse from the hall table and left the

trailer, making sure Cindy was on her way back before heading to her car.

Tori retrieved her favorite stuffed animal, a furry gray platypus. Rachel shook off dirt before she let her daughter hug it to her chest. "Stay on the porch till the car is gone, okay?"

She approached Cindy who'd moseyed back across the highway with her ultra-sexy, phony walk that Rachel disliked.

Wary of her mom's Cheshire cat grin, she asked, "What's up?"

"I've got a date," Cindy said with a whole boatload of smugness.

Disappointment thrummed through Rachel. So that's the kind of man Travis was, a guy who kissed strangers, but liked flashy women like Cindy. Was the man a player? Had she pegged him all wrong? "When?"

"Tonight."

"Tonight? But I'm working. You're taking care of Tori."

"I know. I'll ask Laurie to babysit for a few hours." Cindy went to the porch and bent to talk to Tori. "You don't mind, do you, honey? Laurie is fun."

"She colors with me." Tori smiled with Cindy's dimples.

"But I can't afford to pay her," Rachel objected, knowing Cindy wouldn't offer to pick up the tab.

"Sure you can. You make good tips at the bar."

"But—" What could she say? *I need money to move out, to get away from you?* She couldn't bear to sound so cold and ungrateful, especially not when Cindy had been kind enough to take her in. Rachel should have never moved back into the trailer with Cindy and her resentment, but what else could she have done? Davey had left her with nothing but broken promises and hot air.

Rachel gave in to the inevitable. "Okay. I'll be home after one."

Before leaving, Rachel kissed Tori again because, while Davey hadn't been able to keep a buck in his pocket, he had made her laugh a lot and had given her the most precious of gifts, two children.

Just as Rachel opened her car door, Tori called, "See you later, aggilator."

Ah, Victoria, my sweet divine daughter, you raise my spirits as much as your father used to.

Rachel blew her an air kiss. "Alligator, Tori-ori-ori-o. In a while, crocodile," she sang and got into her old car and drove away laughing, but not before catching her new neighbor watching her with a strange expression on his face.

Travis Read, who are you? The man who loved his carousel ride this morning, or the kind who is attracted to a flashy, shallow flirt like my mother?

A HEADACHE POUNDED behind Rachel's left eye. The tray full of beers she carried dragged down her arms. Was the music louder than usual tonight?

Honey's Place was the only bar in Rodeo. True, there was the diner, but her friend Vy ran an alcohol-free eatery, and most people wanted beer with their fries on a Friday night.

A lot of these people were cowboys who worked the ranches in the area. They came in at the end of the week for liquor, great burgers and fun music.

Despite her aching legs and feet, Rachel hustled. She needed her tips, needed to come up with an alternative plan now that Abigail's house had been sold.

If she felt a tad desperate, well…she was.

A table called for a round of beers. Rachel headed to the bar to fill the order.

"How're you doing?" Rushed but efficient, Honey Armstrong filled orders as quickly as her servers brought them to the bar. Her mane of long, blond curls wild tonight, she peered at Rachel critically. "You look tired."

Fearful of giving Honey a reason to send her home early, Rachel put on her game face.

"I'm good."

"Rach, don't try to fool me. You know you can't."

"I'll take a dinner break soon," Rachel promised.

Honey pointed a finger at her. "You'd better. You look worn out."

It was Friday night, the bar was packed and Rachel needed to hustle. She would take care of her aching body tomorrow morning.

Off-duty, Sheriff Cole Payette, sidled up to the bar and sat on the only empty stool. His spot. No matter how busy Honey's got, the locals left it empty for him. Friday and Saturday nights often found him sitting there for hours, nursing a beer.

Rachel liked him.

As it turned out, Rachel didn't get that break she'd promised Honey she would take. Her energy flagged, but customers continued to pour in.

With every step, her feet screamed for attention.

Too bad. As long as there were customers, she would continue to work and bring in tips.

She set a heavy tray of mugs of beer onto the table next to the front door and handed them around. She was just making change when she felt a draft. New arrivals. Good. More tips.

She glanced up…and froze. Cindy walked in with Travis, the man freshly shaved and movie-star handsome, the tips of his hair still damp from a shower, she guessed.

Why couldn't Cindy have taken him to the diner for dinner? Why come here? But Rachel knew. Her mom was showing off that she was with the handsome new cowboy in town, and Honey's would be a lot more crowded than the diner. Cindy liked an audience.

She wore even more spangles tonight and had put on her sparkly eye shadow.

When he saw Rachel, Travis raised one eyebrow as if to ask, "You work here?"

Rachel suppressed the part of herself that found him attractive.

Fantasizing about a handsome stranger when she looked like a beer barrel on legs was just the type of day-dreaming she had to quit.

Anyhow, Cindy must be his type. He'd asked her out on a date pretty darn quickly, hadn't he? Which meant he wasn't Rachel's type. And why was she having those kinds of unlikely thoughts, anyway? He was dating Cindy, and he had bought Rachel's house. Cindy was welcome to him.

Rachel's dating days were long over.

Then why, in the middle of a crowded bar surrounded by people she'd grown up with and loved, did Rachel feel so lonely? So in need of someone to talk to? Of someone who would listen? Or who would just hold her hand so she didn't feel desperately alone?

Travis and Cindy sat at one of her tables, and Rachel left them with menus while she finished delivering drinks to another couple of tables.

When she returned, she pointed to the hooks lining the walls on either side of the door. "You can hang your hat there."

Travis raised his eyebrows. "I didn't notice them. No one will take it?"

Rachel's grin might have been tired, but she dredged up a ghost of this morning's sass. He needed to understand what kind of town he'd moved to.

"Not in this town. A man's hat is sacred around these parts. All the establishments in town have their cowboy hat hooks."

"Thanks. I'll keep it in mind."

"What can I get for you two?"

"A gin and tonic and a bacon burger with fries," Cindy said.

"I'll take a Corona," Travis said, "with an order of the hottest wings you got, a bacon double cheeseburger and a side of onion rings. You have coleslaw?"

Rachel nodded.

"Creamy?"

"Sharp vinaigrette."

"The way I like it. I'll take a side of that, too."

The way she liked it, too. "I'll make sure it's slurpy." She smiled.

Travis's returning smile might have been small, but moonbeams dazzled.

Get your head out of the clouds, Rachel.

Cindy sniffed.

After Rachel picked up the menus and walked away, she heard Travis say, "She looks tired. Is she okay?"

"She's fine. She's tougher than she looks."

So are you, Mom. Tough as nails. She bit down on that thought. It was uncharitable. Mom had a right to her fun, but Rachel was filled with jealousy, a mean-spirited emotion unworthy of her, but undeniable. She wouldn't mind sitting down for a carefree evening in a bar for drinks and a burger with a handsome man.

Hey, you chose your life. You need to live it without regrets.

A good philosophy, just hard to hold on to when she was dog-tired.

Chapter Four

Travis delivered his hat to the row of hooks on the wall at the front of Honey's Place.

Cowboy hat after cowboy hat graced the wall, most in muted blacks and tans, but a couple in white. Seemed to be the only kind of hat here.

He glanced around at the Western decor with its twin themes of old and new. Big old wagon wheels lined the walls along with huge modern landscapes of local scenery, not overly sentimental stuff, but rugged and true to nature. Local artist, maybe?

Hundreds of white fairy lights illuminated the rafters.

The people were loud, but Travis heard not one discordant note, just a lot of folks having a good time. The huge space rang with laughter. Denim and Western shirts abounded, along with plenty of silver jewelry on the women. He didn't doubt a good portion of the hats on the wall belonged to those same women.

My kind of town.

A country and western band belted out hits from a small stage at the back end of the long room. He tapped his fingers on his thighs.

He returned to the small table Cindy had chosen, a table that fit only two, snugly. She'd said they were meeting up with a bunch of her friends.

"So where are the friends we're supposed to meet?"

Travis asked. He had to make sure she got his message loud and clear. This wasn't a date.

He wasn't looking for romance. Besides, she wasn't his kind of woman at all.

"They'll be along soon," she said, her gaze darting about the bar and her knee doing a quick jig. "Do you dance?"

Before he could respond, she was hauling him out of his seat and to the dance floor where they joined a crowd of line dancers moving to a Brooks and Dunn cover.

Just as the second song started, he spotted Rachel carrying a tray of food and drinks to their table. He dragged Cindy off the dance floor. "I'm starving. Let's eat."

When Rachel put the tray down, it wobbled. He ran to grab it.

"I'm okay," she said, but his beer tipped over the edge and landed on the floor. The bottle shattered, sending suds all over his boots.

Rachel gasped. "I'm so sorry," she whispered. "I'll clean it up." She rushed away.

He still held the tray with the food. He spread the plates and Cindy's drink on their table, and left the empty tray on the bar.

"Rachel's always been clumsy." Cindy looked unhappy. Thunderclouds formed on what had been a clear evening. Travis didn't know what went on between these two women. The last place he needed to be was stuck in the middle.

"The tray was heavy. No problem. A little beer never hurt a pair of boots." He waggled his eyebrows comically to ease Cindy's pique. "These've survived a hell of a lot worse."

Cindy seemed to relax.

Rachel returned with a broom and mop, her stomach leading the way. "I'll get you another beer, but I need to clean this up before someone slips and falls."

"You go get the beer. I'll do this." He tried to take the broom away from her, but she held on.

"Nope." Rachel shot him a look of grim determination. "It's my job."

"I don't mind. I can do it."

"No." The woman had a strong grip, and even stronger willpower.

Travis let go, and she swept up the glass.

"You look pale. You okay?"

Her back stiffened as though maybe he'd offended her. *Note to self. Don't show this woman pity.*

"I'm peachy," she said, struggling to smile, but tense lines bracketed her mouth.

The sexy good humor he'd found so attractive this morning had crawled home to bed early, leaving behind an exhausted shell.

Someone called from another table. "Rachel, we need another round here."

"Be right there, Lester." She rushed to the bar and placed their order, returned with Travis's beer, then disappeared into the back. A minute later, she returned with a freshly rinsed mop and finished cleaning up. Then she hurried to the bar and picked up a full tray of drinks.

Head spinning from the whirlwind, Travis asked, "You worry about her at all?"

Cindy sighed. "Yeah, I do, but she chose to marry a lazy loser. Whatever trouble she's in, she brought on herself." She pointed a French fry at him. "Before you start thinking I'm heartless, I took her back in after her husband died."

"Shame he died. Man, that's tough." He couldn't imagine how hard it would have been for his sister if her husband had died before Colt was born.

Cindy nodded. "I babysit her daughter when she's working."

"Except for tonight."

"I needed a night out." He'd put her on the defensive.

Careful to keep censure out of his voice, he asked quietly, "There are no friends coming, are there?" She'd assured him she was meeting people, and he was welcome to join them. The woman had misrepresented the evening.

"No." She smiled with the barest hint of hope in her eyes. "Being out with me isn't so bad, is it?"

"No, it isn't." Which was mainly true. Cindy had a lot of perky energy. "I gotta be honest, Cindy. I'm not looking for romance. I just need to get settled in. This isn't an official date." He softened it with a smile. "It's good to be out on a Friday night with a pretty woman, though."

Mollified, she sipped her drink.

Just after he'd taken a bite of an excellent charred bacon double cheeseburger, a hand settled onto his shoulder. It belonged to Artie Hanson from the auto shop.

"Brought the keys to your truck." He dropped them onto the table in front of Travis's plate, axle grease ground into every crack and wrinkle of his clean hands. "It's sitting in front of the shop."

Travis had phoned Artie to make sure the mechanic could finish the work by tonight so he'd be spared the ride home with Cindy. He liked to be independent.

Travis swallowed. "That's great, man. Thanks." He reached for his wallet. "How much do I owe you?"

Artie waved it away. "Boss lets me off duty on Friday nights." The man laughed. An inside joke. He owned the shop. He could set his own hours. "You going to be in town on the weekend? Stop in and settle the bill then. Or on Monday."

Artie clapped his back and walked away.

"Is he always so trusting?"

"Most people in this town are." Cindy's tone was only half admiring. The other half sounded resentful to Travis's ear, but he wasn't about to ask why.

While he ate, his gaze roamed the bar. He stopped when he realized he was keeping an eye on Rachel.

She's no concern of yours.

It seemed that the habit of caring for others, after years of taking care of Samantha, was ground into him. *Quit it.*

He'd finished his burger, wings and onion rings, all while Rachel's steps slowed and her face grew paler.

Not your business, man. Let it go.

He couldn't. He fought the urge to help. It didn't matter. Guess he'd spent too many years taking care of his younger sister to see a woman go so far into a bad case of hurt without helping her. He had to do something.

He excused himself and walked to the bar where he squeezed in between two old guys drinking whiskey. Behind the bar, a beauty hustled to fill drink orders. This town sure had a lot of pretty women. A mass of curly blond hair flowed down the bartender's back to her waist.

"Hey, you're Travis, aren't you?" she asked. Laughter lurked in her china-doll blue eyes. At his surprised look, she answered his unspoken question. "It's a small town. Everyone knows your name by now. I'm Honey, by the way."

Ah. The owner.

Friendly smile as well as pretty. Nice. He handed her a twenty. "Can I order a burger or something for Rachel? She needs a break."

Honey's gaze sought out Rachel. Her lips compressed.

"She still hasn't stopped? Honestly, that girl. Talk about being stubborn." Honey removed a towel from her shoulder and tossed it onto the bar. "I told her to take a break well over an hour ago. If she's not careful, she'll hurt my future godchild."

While Travis went back to the table, she slipped from behind the bar into the back hallway.

"Honey's gone to get Rachel some food," he told Cindy. He figured he should explain why he'd left.

Cindy cocked her head to one side. "You're a nice man, aren't you? That was a real kind thing to do."

Since he'd told her it was good to be out with a pretty woman, Cindy's mood had mellowed some. The second gin and tonic helped, too.

A guy got up from the bar and walked behind to pull mugs of draft and fill orders while Honey was gone.

"Who's that customer who's serving drinks now?" he asked Cindy.

She checked out the bar. "Cole Payette. He likes to help Honey sometimes."

"I hope I didn't get Rachel into trouble with her boss." He finished his beer.

"Honey's her friend," Cindy said. "She won't fire Rachel."

A few minutes later, Honey returned to the big room with an order of chicken fingers and fries and handed them to Rachel. She pointed to Travis, probably telling Rachel who'd paid for them.

Rachel shot him a look full of brimstone. Oh, shit. Clasping her hands behind her back, she refused to take the plate from Honey. The gesture made her stomach stick out a mile.

She stormed over to their table. "I don't know why you think you can tell me when I should be eating. I can figure out my own breaks."

"Sorry, I—"

"Of all the paternalistic, presumptuous things to do. I don't need your charity. Go buy dinner for someone else."

He shot his hands in front of himself, palms out. "I didn't mean to offend," he said. "You're looking more exhausted with every step. Considering how early it was when I saw you at the carousel this morning, you've put in a long day already and this bar doesn't close for another few hours."

Beside him, Honey gasped. She planted a fist on her hip. "You were out there this morning? You get one morning a week to sleep in, and you spent it at the fairground?"

Rachel's mulish expression turned chagrined. "I put the carousel to bed for the winter." She shot Travis a look that said, "Thanks a lot for snitching on me."

Honey forced the plate of food into Rachel's hands. "We'll have our fund-raising dance in a couple of weeks, and then we'll forget about it until spring. Got it? I know the fairground is important to you, but take it easy for a while. Take care of yourself." Her voice had softened. "Go eat."

"Ma'am," Travis said to Rachel, "I'm real sorry I made presumptions where I shouldn't have. I don't make the same mistake twice." He wouldn't do it again. She had a valid point. He had no right to tell her anything. She wasn't his baby sister.

"Would you consider eating the meal because it's hot and ready to go? No sense wasting it." Travis watched the moment she realized he was right.

"Okay. Thanks." She sounded begrudging, but took the food anyway, and that was the important thing.

Honey pointed toward the back where Travis assumed the restrooms were. Rachel headed there with the plate of chicken. Honey took Rachel's tray and filled her orders.

Rachel disappeared around a corner.

The guy named Cole kept filling orders at the bar while Honey took trays of drinks around.

Travis asked where the washrooms were and Cindy told him. He used the restroom, then returned down the hallway toward the bar. He stopped when he passed an open doorway and backtracked. Inside a cramped office, Rachel sat on a plastic chair, wolfing down the food. He hadn't noticed her the first time through the hallway.

"I hope I didn't get you into trouble," he said from the doorway.

She startled, her gold-flecked eyes huge and framed by gray bruises of exhaustion. The poor woman wasn't just tired. She was plumb worn thin enough to see through.

"No. Honey's a good friend." She took a bite of a chicken finger. "You were right. Both of you. I was struggling. Thank you for the food."

Travis hid a smile with one hand. She was saying all the right things, but her tone said she still resented being told what to do.

He could relate to that.

Beside her sat a pint of milk and a plastic food container filled with something beige dotted with bits of color.

"What's that?" he asked.

"What's what?"

"That stuff." He pointed to the plastic container.

"Quinoa salad."

Shaking his head, Travis leaned against the doorjamb. "You and my sister. She likes that weird California health stuff, too."

Rachel laughed, a musical counterpoint to the noise from the bar behind him.

She had a good laugh, clean and without guile. "Quinoa's not from California. It's South American, but yeah, it is healthy."

"It's beige. Does it taste as bland as it looks?"

She shook her head. "It's good."

Her worn brown cowboy boots sat on the floor next to the chair. Cracks in the leather attested to their age. Through her thin socks, her ankles looked too big for such a small woman. "Your feet swell up?"

"When I'm on them too long. It's the pregnancy."

If she were his sister, he would massage them for her. He used to when Sammy was pregnant with the boys and her husband was too busy navel-gazing to pay her much attention. He sensed Rachel wouldn't appreciate a stranger touching her feet, or offering sympathy.

Nor did he have any desire to touch her again after the foolishness of this afternoon's kiss.

She looked hesitant and then seemed to gather courage. "What's it like inside these days?"

Huh? He stared at her. "What's what like?"

"The house. What shape is it in? I haven't been in for a long time. The owner was in palliative care for the past year."

She liked his house that much? "Not great. I've got a lot of work to do to bring it up to scratch."

"That bad?"

"Nothing impossible." Her wistful tone puzzled him. "It's just a house."

"Just a house?" she squeaked. "It's beautiful. It's got great bones and huge potential. Even with the work that needs to be done, it's perfect." She looked so damn cute with her warm eyes and thick eyelashes and tawny braid with wisps of hair floating around her cheeks. They were filling with color now that she was off her feet and eating.

He didn't like this attraction. It made him antsy and tense. He started to back out of the room, but she asked, "Hardwood floors still in good shape?"

"They need refinishing. Oak. Three-quarter inch. They'll be incredible once they're done." Travis had a good feeling about this house for his family, if he could get the work done by Christmas. "You should see the fireplace with the carved wooden mantel."

In her smile, he saw longing. "Still beautiful?"

"A work of art. Looks like I've got to strip off about twelve coats of paint, though. From all of the moldings, too." He cocked his head. "You seem to know the place well."

She smiled, and it was sweet and wholesome. "The owner was a special friend. Before she became ill, we had tea together a lot."

She swallowed and looked away. He thought it was sadness choking her up.

Unsure what drove him other than a need to reassure her

about himself and her mother, because it felt weird to be attracted to the daughter, even if he didn't want to be, while having drinks with the mother, he said, "It isn't a date."

Her hand paused on the way to her mouth, one lonely French fry dangling from her fingers. "What?"

"With your mom? Cindy? Tonight isn't a date. She said we were meeting other folks. I thought I could get to know some townspeople."

She chewed her fry with a small, thoughtful frown furrowing her brow. Another aspect he liked. She had depth, this one.

"I'll meet ranch hands while I work, but not enough of every kind of person living here. My family—"

A gasp from the doorway caught his attention, and he glanced behind him. Cindy.

"What are you two doing?" Disappointment hovered beneath her suspicious anger.

Travis really didn't have time for drama.

"Shooting the breeze," he said in the most casual tone he could muster. He owed this woman nothing. He could talk to whomever he wanted, but he didn't want to make trouble between mother and daughter. "Just getting to know one of my neighbors."

Cindy spun away and slammed into the women's washroom. Talk about being high maintenance.

"Am I in trouble?" he asked.

Rachel's animation about the house leached out of her. "We're both in trouble. Cindy can hold a grudge for days. You'd better go back to your table and make it up to her."

Travis sighed. Was one night of peace and innocent fun too much to expect?

Just as he left the room, Rachel stopped him. "She's not a bad person, honest. She's just…" She shrugged.

Just real needy. "Got it."

Throughout the rest of the evening, he managed to smooth Cindy's ruffled feathers, not really sure why he was bothering. He didn't know the woman and didn't care whether she nursed a good pout, but he thought of Rachel and wondered how Cindy's anger would affect her.

Shortly after ten, a fight broke out. Travis didn't know who the two guys were, or what their beefs were, but they came too close to his table. When one of them bumped into Rachel serving nearby, he got up and steadied her, holding a hand up to let the guy know to keep his distance.

The guy could barely stand upright, wavering on his drunken feet and grinning idiotically.

The man who'd taken over for Honey earlier at the bar came running, grabbing the second guy by the scruff of his neck and propelling him against the wall with one of the guy's arms shoved behind him and halfway up his back.

"Goddamn it, Clint," Cole yelled above the driving beat of the music. "I told you before. You and Jamie need to keep your fights out of public places. You want to fight, take it home."

He whipped a pair of handcuffs out of his back pocket and cuffed the guy. Travis stared.

Cole turned to the man Travis held off with his raised right hand. Three sheets to the wind, he burped up a lungful of beer and chicken wings.

"Do I need to cuff you, too, Jamie?"

"Naw. I'm okay now. I'll go home peacefully."

"And you, Clint? Should I call out one of the deputies? You wanna spend the night in jail?"

Clint shook his head. "I'll leave."

Cole unlocked the cuffs, then watched the pair of them stumble out, leaning on each other like the best of buddies.

The man stuck out his hand. "Cole Payette. I'm sheriff here. You're the new guy."

Travis nodded and shook his hand. "Travis Read. What was their problem?"

"Brothers from different mothers. Every so often they

take potshots at each other, but only when they're drunk. The rest of the time, they're good buddies."

Payette righted a chair that had been knocked over, watching Travis with an odd smile.

"Good to meet you, Travis. Welcome to Rodeo. Usually we're a peaceful town. Thanks for your help." Cole's eyes slid off to Travis's left and then back to him. He grinned and returned to his stool at the bar.

"Um… Travis?"

The voice so close beside him startled him. Travis looked down at Rachel. "Yeah?"

"You can let go of me now."

Cripes. The whole time he'd held off the guy named Jamie, he'd held Rachel with his other arm, tucked against his body and out of harm's way.

"Oh…sorry…ah, I—" He didn't know what to say because he didn't know what he'd been thinking.

A small handful, a perfect fit, her belly hard and warm against him, she belonged in his arms.

It felt natural and good to hold her.

No! No, no, no. He didn't need a woman in his life right now, especially not one laden with burdens he didn't want to bear.

He didn't want to like her.

A funny smile curled her lips. "I truly can take care of myself, Travis. I deal with stuff like this most nights."

At least she wasn't mad at him.

"I really didn't know I was doing that."

"I know. I could tell."

The feeling of well-being, and the sense of rightness she engendered in him, shook him so badly he rushed to let her go.

Before he could, the softest of touches flitted across his ribs. Wonder filled him. The touch had come from Rachel's big belly.

"What was that?"

Despite her obvious fatigue, this morning's mischievous grin made an appearance.

"That was the baby," she said. "Beth."

"No fooling?"

"No fooling, Travis. Guess she was saying hello."

It happened again. Wild. Amazing. That little creature inside that big bump was real and moving. "What was it? A hand or a foot?"

"Could have been. Or an elbow. Maybe a knee." She ran her hand over her belly. "It's pretty awesome, isn't it?"

The baby moved again, some incredibly tiny part of her body brushing across him, like maybe the little thing was communicating with him. Saying hi. Touching. Reaching out. Whoo.

"It's…it's incredible." He didn't have words to describe the feeling. Whoo-hoo. It was about the most magical experience imaginable.

He released Rachel by increments, because he was also letting go of another creature, her baby. He'd never much thought about how real babies were before birth.

He'd only met Rachel a mere twelve or so hours ago, but she'd now bestowed on him two wondrous gifts—a child's dream ride on a carousel, and an unborn baby's touch.

"I'd better get back to work," she said.

He bent to pick up the tray she'd dropped, handing it to her with his mouth open and searching for words. There were none.

Had Cole's funny smile been about Travis holding Rachel as if she belonged to him? She didn't. No woman did. Uh-uh. No way, no how. He had one priority—to take care of his sister and nephews and then hightail it away from here.

While he might be filled with awe, he would never think to take on the encumbrance of parenthood for himself. More power to her, but he was hunky-dory on his own.

He returned to Cindy. It was time to head home.

It took them a while to leave the bar because everyone and his uncle wanted an introduction. Friendly people. Considering the night a success, he left knowing that Sammy and her boys would find a community in Rodeo where they could belong.

He caught a last glimpse of Rachel, who was too busy to notice him leaving.

Cindy dropped him off at the garage to pick up his truck. He scooted out of her pickup the second it stopped. He wasn't about to give Cindy ideas about kissing goodnight.

Once he'd driven himself to the house, he wandered the too-quiet rooms. The echo of his boots in the stillness set up an emptiness in him that rankled.

Boots. On a wood floor.

He needed to become more refined. No carting of muck and God knew what else into his new home. This wasn't a bunkhouse. It was Sammy's new home.

He returned to the front door and took them off.

Tired, he entered his bedroom and made up his new bed with the sheets he'd had delivered. He unpacked his saddlebags, his belongings paltry enough, his lifestyle so simple it took him all of ten minutes to put away his clothes. He stared at the freshly made bed. He might be bone weary, but his mind wouldn't quit. He knew he wouldn't sleep, so there was no point trying.

He unloaded a bunch of new kid's books onto the new bookshelves.

The house was too quiet. He hated the hollowness of the place. He'd have to get a TV soon, or a radio—anything to fill the emptiness until the boys arrived.

Christmas and his nephews couldn't come soon enough.

Chapter Five

At seven on Saturday morning, Travis walked down Rodeo's Main Street, humming with energy and feeling so darn lucky that he'd found this town for his family.

Despite Cindy's subterfuge, last night had been good. He'd met a few people and had fun.

Passing one small shop after another, with names like Jorgenson's Hardware and Hiram's Pharmacy and Nelly's 'Dos 'n' Don'ts, unpretentious and without a trace of neon lights or razzle-dazzle, he knew he'd made the right choice in buying a house for Samantha here.

He had simple needs. He'd had nothing much to spend his paychecks on once he'd put Samantha through school. The money was just sitting in the bank. He'd put it down on a house for Sammy and the boys.

They were his only family.

Funny that he'd never thought to discuss repayment with Sammy. If she did, she did. If she didn't, well, hell, so what? What did he need a house for?

When he felt a trace of yearning on his own behalf, he ignored it.

He returned his attention to the town.

Cowboy hats and worn-in denim were everywhere, on both men and women. Not a single pair of designer jeans could be found.

Pickup trucks lined the road—not urban warriors, but

real honest-to-God working vehicles covered with rust, dust and dirt. This was a working town.

He nodded to an old man passing by with the bowlegged gait of a retired cowhand.

Travis stepped into the Summertime Diner for breakfast. He'd picked up a few groceries yesterday, but he wanted to be out among people. Eating breakfast alone in the house didn't appeal to him. He was used to eating in farmhouse kitchens surrounded by ranch hands or cooking up bacon and eggs in a bunkhouse with a bunch of other men. Udall vouched for the diner, so here he was.

Busy place, even this early on a Saturday.

Looking to his left, he spotted wooden hooks lined with cowboy hats. He added his to the mix. It was a funny tradition this town had, but seeing his hat hanging with so many others made him feel like he was part of something.

If that also struck a chord of loneliness in him—the awareness that he really had no community—so be it. Part of his life.

All of the stools at the counter were already occupied. Too bad. That was usually a good place to strike up a conversation and get to know people.

Spotting an empty booth near the back, he headed for it, catching a waitress's eye and pantomiming that he wanted coffee. He fell into the booth facing the street. Might as well get a look at the local color.

A small voice in the booth behind him said, "Mommy, I want pamcakes."

"Okay, sweetie-pie. Pancakes it is. Blueberry?"

He recognized Rachel's upbeat voice. She must be here with her daughter. Awfully early for her to be out, considering she closed the bar last night.

"Yeah. Booberry," the pip-squeak said.

"*Blue*berry."

The child giggled. "I said *boo*berry." That childish

voice, that high-pitched laugh made him ache to see his nephews. Soon.

A family entered the diner and searched for an empty table. There were none left, and here he sat hogging an entire booth to himself.

He didn't want to sit with Rachel. He didn't like that he found her attractive. He didn't like that he'd thought about her as soon as he woke up in the house she'd been angry with him for buying.

The family's kids looked antsy, as though maybe they were hungry.

He couldn't invite them to join him. There were too many of them.

He gave in as graciously as he could, unsure whether Rachel would even agree, and peeked around the backrest.

"Good morning," he said.

Rachel didn't look surprised to see him. She must have seen him enter the restaurant.

"Hi," she said.

"Place is filling up." He gestured over his shoulder. "There's a family looking for a booth. You mind if I give them mine and share yours?"

She didn't bat an eye, as though this kind of thing happened regularly. "Sure thing," she said. "Tori, scoot on over along the bench. Travis is going to join us."

Travis gestured to the family standing by the front door that they could have the booth. They dazzled him with their gratitude.

In Rachel's booth, the little one moved over and Travis joined them.

"I'm Tori!" the pip-squeak said. "I'm having pamcakes."

"Me, too."

"What kind are you having?"

"Booberry!" he said, feeling foolish, but gratified when she giggled.

"Mommy," she squealed. "Travis calls them booberry, too."

Rachel caught his eye and smiled. It did wonders for her face, softening that strong jaw and warming the whiskey highlights in her eyes.

The child picked up a raggedy plush animal. A platypus?

"This is Puss. You can kiss him." She held the thing up to his face. He kissed it on the nose while his cheeks heated like hot tar on an August afternoon.

Watching his discomfort, Rachel grinned, some of yesterday morning's sass returning after a night's sleep. Travis settled back against the bench and steeled his heart, or libido, or whatever it was causing this strong unwanted appeal.

She looked younger this morning with her hair pulled up in a high ponytail.

The waitress arrived with a coffeepot and orange juice in a plastic cup for Tori.

Rachel put her hand over her cup. "Vy, when you have a minute, can you bring decaf?"

"Sure thing, Rachel. I forgot. What'll you folks have to eat?"

After the waitress left to place their orders, Travis asked, "Does the owner make her dress up like someone out of the forties because it's a diner or something?"

Vy wore a kerchief on her head, black eyeliner that curved up at the corners and bright red lipstick to match a red-checked shirt. Her black skirt flared out like a bell, swishing around legs accentuated by a pair of wedged heels. Or he thought that was what they were called.

"Vy *is* the owner, and that's just her style. She likes to dress retro."

"Seems out of place in a boots and denim town."

"Yeah. She likes the surprise value. Tourists think it's fun."

Travis drank half of his coffee and started to feel human

again. "You worked late last night. What brings you out so early today?"

"Gramma doesn't like noise in the morning," Tori answered. "Mommy brings me here for brekfest."

The child rose up onto her knees, picked up her OJ and took a sip. "Only sometimes, though." She set the juice down with exaggerated care, without spilling a drop.

"Only Saturday," Rachel confirmed. "It's too expensive to eat out every day."

So, Cindy was sleeping in while the woman who'd worked until 1:00 a.m. was up at six with her child. He had to hand it to Rachel. She took her job as a mother seriously. She didn't seem resentful or angry, just took quiet responsibility for her daughter.

What did she do for herself? Besides give strangers rides on a carousel she'd fixed up?

Or was she like Sammy, a single mother so fixated on doing the best for her kids that she put her own needs last?

Rachel wiped a dribble of juice from Tori's chin. "Don't let Cindy hear you call her Grandma. She doesn't like it."

"But she is my gramma."

"She is. She just doesn't want to be called that."

"But Carol-Sue can call *her* gramma *Gramma*. Why can't I?"

"Who's Carol-Sue?" Travis asked.

"A character in one of Tori's books."

To her daughter, she said, "Everyone's different. Cindy doesn't like being called Grandma."

Rachel caught his eye. "Cindy loves being a grandmother."

"Gramma loves me."

"Yes, she does, sweetie-pie, but being called Grandma makes her feel old."

Vy returned with pots of both regular and decaf, topping up Travis's mug and filling Rachel's empty cup.

"Thanks, Vy."

Tori hummed beside him and colored on her paper place mat with three crayons.

"May I ask you a question?" Rachel asked.

"Go ahead," he answered. "Won't guarantee I'll answer it, but ask away." He craved privacy, especially after a childhood of being on the receiving end of too much gossip.

"Why would a single man buy that Victorian? I would have pegged you for a ranch house kind of guy."

"You'd be right about that, but I bought it for my sister and her two sons."

She smiled suddenly, brilliantly. "That's okay, then."

"What do you mean?"

"That house deserves a family. It should be full of children and happiness."

Her selflessness—she even put a house's needs before her own!—rattled him, maybe because she accepted her burdens with grace while he itched to be free, with nothing more on his mind than a good ride over a green field.

Even if he wished that he and Sammy had had a mother half as committed as Rachel, resentment bubbled. Was the woman a saint?

"It's just a house, Rachel."

She didn't seem to notice the hard edge to his voice.

The longing, the wistfulness he'd seen in her last night when they talked about his house painted her cheeks pink.

"Children will live there. That's all that matters."

A burst of intuition hit him, or maybe it was the slight hint of rancor in her tone.

"Should have been your children? Right?"

"Yeah." She sounded bitter. "In a perfect world."

The flash of unhappiness on her face vanished in an instant. The woman was resilient.

"Again, why the Victorian?" she asked. "Why not the Podchuk ranch house? It's up for sale."

Not usually a man for introspection, Travis had asked himself that question a hundred times. "I can't rightly say. It's old-fashioned. I guess it looks like it could make a nice home."

She nodded.

He sipped his coffee, then said, "Can I ask you something?"

Rachel nodded.

"How did your husband die?"

"A accident," the pip-squeak piped up.

He glanced down at the child. Damn. He'd forgotten she was there, or he wouldn't have asked. "I'm real sorry about that."

"He rided a motorcycle and wented too fast and hitted a tree."

Aaaahhh. Hence the deep concern he'd seen on Rachel's face when he'd tipped his bike yesterday. He'd recognized something more, though. Anger.

"Motorcycles is bad," Tori said. "Really bad."

Travis glanced at Rachel but she'd shut down, her hazel eyes blank, as though she'd pulled blinds down. The windows to her soul weren't sharing anything with him. Both resentment and anger at her late husband churned through Travis. It was all well and good for him to ride, but he didn't have dependents. Rachel's husband should have behaved more responsibly.

But was Travis truly free? What about Sammy and his nephews? Now that Sammy's husband had farted off to the Himalayas to *find himself* and she had a crook like her former boss on her tail, weren't she and the boys his responsibility? Wasn't he the only person they could depend on? Was *he* being careless when he rode his bike? What if something happened to him? What would Sammy do?

Maybe he'd park it in the garage for a while and just use the truck. Next week, he'd take out a life insurance policy on himself with Sammy as the beneficiary.

Man, why hadn't he thought to do it months ago?

"Tell me about your sister," Rachel said.

Travis rubbed the back of his neck. He didn't share, not like Sammy who blurted out every thought.

Still, Rachel seemed genuinely curious, not prying, and not one to spread gossip.

"She's six years younger than me. Thirty-one. Our Mom died of cancer when she was only twelve. Dad had died the year before. I was eighteen, so she never went to a foster home."

No need to mention he figured the big C had been floating out in the atmosphere looking for the most tired, sorriest woman around and had found Cerise Read. Once it took hold, she'd succumbed quickly. Dad had died the year before of cirrhosis of the liver.

"But it did mean you were a teenage boy taking care of your sister." Rachel cut to the heart of the matter. "Must have been hard. No time for yourself, I'm guessing?"

Travis nodded. "It was just the two of us for years until Sammy got married and had her two boys, now nine and five."

"She and her boys are coming here? Husband, too?"

"Nope. Sammy's divorced. Her ex is off in a Hindu temple in the Himalayas somewhere." For all intents and purposes, Travis was their stand-in father.

When their breakfasts came, he dug in, but put down his fork when Rachel reached across the table to cut up Tori's pancakes.

"Let me," he said. "It's easier from this side of the table."

Having spent time with his nephews, he knew how small to make the pieces and how much syrup to pour on, or how much *not* to. "My nephews like to drown their pancakes in syrup and their fries in ketchup."

"Mommy, Travis got sausages. I don't got sausages."

"I didn't order any for you, honey. I didn't know you would want them. Besides, you won't be able to finish your pancakes if you have something else with them."

"Uh-huh. I can. I want sausages."

"Okay." Rachel raised her hand to flag the waitress, Vy, but Travis stopped her.

"Why don't I give her one of mine? She won't eat a whole order of sausages. If she can't finish her pancakes, I'll eat them."

"You don't mind?"

"No, ma'am. I'm used to sharing with my nephews."

"What's nephews?" the pip-squeak asked while Travis sliced a sausage first lengthwise, then crosswise into small bits and put them on her plate.

Rachel explained the concept of nephews.

"What's their names?" Tori stuffed two pieces of pancake into her mouth. Travis wiped the syrup from the corners of her lips.

"Jason and Colt."

"Do they like Carol-Sue books? She gots a dog *and* a cat."

Travis smiled. "Somehow I doubt those boys are reading about a girl named Carol-Sue."

"What are they like?" Rachel asked, and Travis was off and running on his favorite subject outside horses.

He exhausted the subject of his nephews. To her credit, Rachel didn't look bored. Neither did Tori, who kept asking questions about them. Curious kid.

After breakfast, they stepped out of the restaurant. Remembering last night's fiasco with Rachel's dinner, Travis didn't make the mistake of denting her pride by offering to pay for breakfast. They settled their own bills.

Before Travis could go his own way, the pip-squeak took hold of his hand and started to drag him down Main.

"Travis, come on. I got to show you something."

"Tori, no," Rachel protested. "I'm sure Travis has stuff to do."

"But, Mommy—"

"No, Victoria. Leave Travis alone."

The child looked so crestfallen that Travis asked, "What does she want to show me?"

Rachel sighed. "A pair of boots she wants. She checks every Saturday to make sure they're still there."

"Okay," he said. "Let's go."

"Are you sure?"

"It's only five minutes out of my day. Where are they?"

Tori saw which direction the conversation was heading and took hold of his hand again. Rachel shrugged. They followed Tori to the window of a shop that sold Western clothes.

Tori let go of him and pressed her hands and nose against the glass.

"My boots," she whispered, and Travis leaned close.

"Which ones?"

She pointed to a pair of bright pink cowboy boots, probably the tiniest pair he'd ever seen. So damned cute.

"Those sure are pretty cowboy boots."

"Yeah," she breathed. "I want them, but Mommy says we don't got the money."

He heard Rachel groan behind him. "Thanks for airing all of our secrets, Tori," she said with a gentle laugh.

"We got to save our money for Beth." Tori sounded so adult and so accepting that his heart went out to this little girl.

"Your mom is a smart woman," he said.

They parted ways, with Rachel driving out of town while Travis paid Artie for his truck repairs.

Before returning to his truck, he made one more stop, his feet overtaking his better judgment, but there was a method to his madness.

Yesterday morning on the carousel, Rachel had given him a gift unlike anything he'd had in a long time—five spectacular minutes of freedom from weight and responsibility. He'd been carefree and filled with joy.

He needed to balance the scales. He didn't like being beholden.

More than that, he hadn't liked how resigned Rachel's little girl was already to the realities of life. He remembered the same resignation in Sammy when she was little. Give Tori a few more years, for God's sake.

He stepped into the store and asked how much the pink boots in the window cost.

The low price surprised him until he saw them up close. They weren't real leather, but would that matter to a girl who would outgrow them in four or five months?

"You think these might fit a little girl about this tall?" He gestured with his hand in the vicinity of his knees.

"Probably," the clerk responded. "If they don't fit, bring them back. No problem."

He bought them and tossed the bag into the bed of the truck.

Not ten minutes into the drive home, Travis noticed Rachel's car on the side of the road. Empty. Out in the middle of nowhere.

His gut did a nervous jig. He might not want to care too much, but the woman was pregnant and had a small child with her. He remembered last night's swollen ankles. If her car had broken down and she was walking, her feet wouldn't thank her.

In the distance, two dark shadows, one short and the other shorter, trudged toward the horizon. Travis drove on until he came alongside them, slowed and then passed to pull onto the shoulder far enough ahead that he wouldn't cover them with dust.

He got out of the truck and approached.

He didn't like the begrudging acceptance on Rachel's face, a lack of surprise that something had gone wrong for her, or the way Tori's little feet, clad in pink rubber boots with bright purple flowers, scraped the gravel.

"Car broke down?" he asked.

Rachel nodded.

"We been walking *forever*, Travis." Tori's bottom lip trembled. "Mommy can't carry me 'cause Beth is in the way."

Tori spread her hands to be picked up. "Can you carry me?"

"Sure." He settled her into his arms, her weight, her slim limbs and her tiny wrists fragile compared to his sturdy, rough-and-tumble nephews.

"Any idea what's wrong with your car?" he asked Rachel.

"Old age. It does this regularly. I'm pretty sure I need to replace the battery."

"You need to consider getting a new car."

"Yeah." Behind him, she sighed.

He settled Tori into the backseat of his truck and strapped her in.

"She's too tiny to ride without her car seat," Rachel objected.

He knew that from taking care of his nephews, but they were still a ways away from her home. "We're not going far. I'll be careful."

Rachel climbed into the passenger seat, Travis giving her a gentle boost with a hand to her elbow.

Once behind the wheel, he pulled onto the road and Tori immediately observed, "Travis, you don't got no music."

"Don't have, sweetie," Rachel corrected.

"I know, Mommy. Travis don't have no music."

"Any music."

"I *know*. That what's I'm saying, Mommy. He don't have any music. Where's his music?"

Travis laughed, silently, because he didn't know whether Tori's emotions were as fragile as her tiny body. He flicked the radio knob and Taylor Swift's voice filled the cab.

"'Love Story!'" Tori squealed. A second later, in a high sweet warble, she sang, "'Baby, just say yes.'"

He shot an amused glance at her mother. "She knows this song?"

"She knows all the Taylor Swift songs. She loves music. We have the radio on in the car all the time."

Travis studied her tired profile. "You working tonight?"

"Yeah. People are generous on Saturday night. I'll make good tips."

He pulled into the driveway directly across from his own. Cindy stepped out of her front door, dressed to kill with sparkles galore on her Western shirt, and made up to within an inch of her life. Travis glanced at his watch. Not quite ten. Must be gearing up for a hot lunch date or something.

"You took my daughter out this morning?"

Travis didn't miss the bite in Cindy's tone. "No, ma'am. Her car broke down on the highway. I'm just giving her a lift home." No sense mentioning they'd actually had breakfast together. Even if it wasn't by design, Cindy might not like it. He did his best to avoid drama in his life.

He rounded the truck to help Rachel from the passenger seat, but she was already out and lifting Tori from the back.

"Careful!" he admonished.

A rueful grin tugged at the corners of her mouth. "I can lift her. I just can't carry her."

"What are you going to do about your car?"

"Call Artie at the garage and have him tow it."

That would cost her. "I'm handy with an engine. I'll take a look at it."

"I've got some sense with engines, too."

He smiled. "Yeah. The carousel."

When she answered him with a smile, they seemed to share a sweetness he wasn't used to. It unnerved him.

It seemed to do the same for her. The smile slowly fell from her lips. "I'm sure it's just the battery. It's time for a new one."

Travis addressed Cindy. "You think you could watch the little one for a minute while I take Rachel back to her car?"

Cindy nodded. "C'mon, Tori. Let's go inside."

Rachel climbed back into the truck. When they arrived at her car, Travis popped the hood and retrieved jumper cables from the bed of his truck.

"You're a regular Boy Scout, aren't you?"

He checked for sarcasm, but all he noted on her face was appreciation.

"Get in the car and turn it on when I tell you to."

After he'd lined up the truck with her car, he hooked up the cables to the two batteries and got her car started. He instructed her to drive it for twenty minutes before returning home.

"Thanks, but I know that much."

"Yeah, sorry. I guess you would."

He leaned his forearms on the open window well of the driver's door. She smelled like coconuts. Her shampoo, maybe? "You going to be able to catch a nap before you head to work?"

Her smile showcased even white teeth with one slightly crooked eyetooth. The imperfection didn't detract from her looks. Not at all. Her laugh tinkled on the fresh sunny air. "Not likely."

She drove away.

He waited until her car disappeared and he was sure

the thing was still running before driving home and putting her out of his mind.

Neither she nor her daughter nor her unborn baby were any concern of his.

He changed into work clothes and headed out to the Double U to give Dusty a ride. He brought tools with him and picked up a couple of steel posts from Udall's supply. He located and repaired the fence where yesterday's sheep had gotten tangled, pounding the posts deep into the ground. Felt good to have a hammer in his hands again, to use his muscles, to work.

He worried about Rachel.

"Stop it." His voice echoed across the fields.

Dusty snorted as if in agreement.

"Right," Travis said. "I need a woman and a couple of kids like I need a hole in the head."

After a good long ride across the land that left both him and Dusty satisfied, and during which he'd pinpointed a troublesome spot close to a creek, he returned to his house. He made a note to tell Udall where some of his jackleg fence had been flattened by something big. Moose or elk, maybe. It would need to be repaired before the snow set in for the winter, which could be any day now despite the unseasonably mild weather. You just never knew when winter would roar in this close to the Rockies.

He lunched on tuna sandwiches while those tiny pink cowboy boots sat on the sofa, asking him when he was going to give them to the child. What was appropriate?

Confused, he stepped outside and surveyed his land.

His land.

Lord, what a responsibility.

Chapter Six

"Travis," a tiny voice called from across the road. Tori stood on the front porch of the sorry-looking trailer.

Rachel stood on the shoulder, putting out a bag of yard waste.

Travis sauntered over. "Hey."

"Travis! You came to visit!"

Tori jumped down the steps of the porch and fell, landing on her hands and knees in the dirt. She let out a hurt wail.

Rachel started toward her, but Travis was faster. He picked her up and brushed dirt from her pants.

"I hate this place!"

Startled by the vehemence of Rachel's tone, he spun around to stare at her. She looked undone. Defeated.

"I'm sorry," she said, her lips pressed into a thin line. "I shouldn't have said that. It just sure would be nice to live somewhere with a lawn." Her voice took on a wistful note. "And flowers."

Yeah, he guessed maybe this wasn't the ideal place to raise a kid.

"Travis, look." Tori held out her hands with a little sob. The palms were scraped. Gently, he smoothed off the dirt.

When she rested her head on his shoulder with a weary hiccup, his heart just about broke. He thought of those tiny boots. Now was as good a time as any, he guessed.

"Listen," he said to Rachel, "do you have time before you head into work?"

Don't do this, he warned himself, but his heart refused to listen.

"A few hours." Rachel watched him with a furrowed brow.

"Come to the ranch with me," he blurted because, apparently, he didn't have a speck of prudence left. "Let me take Tori for a ride."

"Ride?" He'd caught Tori's attention. Her head shot up. "What kind of ride?"

"On my horse."

Both Rachel's and Tori's eyes widened as though he'd handed them a bouquet of stars. His five-eleven grew to ten feet tall. It warmed him head to toe.

"Do you mean it?" Rachel asked.

"Yeah, I do. Just a gentle ride in the paddock up on Dusty. It won't be dangerous."

"Yes," Rachel answered lickety-split. Maybe she was afraid he'd change his mind.

"Come over to my place. We'll take the truck."

"No, I need to put Tori in her car seat."

Oh, yeah. He should have remembered that himself.

Her husband had died on the road.

He raised his shoulders, thinking. "I guess we could all go in your car?"

Rachel smiled. "Yes. Let's."

He lifted one finger. "Can you give me a minute?"

Returning to his house, he snagged the pink boots and stared down at them, so small in his callused hands. He missed his nephews. The house was too quiet, too empty. He needed to fill his day.

Justifications for his impulsive actions complete, he went back outside.

He crossed back over the road and Tori squealed. "Mommy, look what Travis got!"

A grin split his face, cracking muscles he hadn't used in a good, long while.

"You want to sit down on the step and we'll get these on you?"

Tori rushed to the porch and yanked off her rubber boots. Travis squatted in front of her and helped her on with the cowboy boots, her feet tinier than he ever remembered his nephews' feet being.

"She'll need thicker socks if she's going to walk far in these. They're still a bit big."

Rachel didn't respond. He glanced over his shoulder. She stared at him like she didn't know what to make of all this, or maybe she just didn't trust him.

Yeah, he understood. Why would she?

They'd met…what?…thirty hours ago? She didn't know him from Adam.

He set the little one upright and stood. Tori ran around the yard, taking the boots for a test drive.

Travis shuffled his feet. He didn't know how to talk about anything personal. "Yesterday morning? That carousel ride?"

She nodded.

"It was a gift." Lord, he felt foolish and awkward saying that.

Her shoulders rose. "It was only a ride, Travis."

"These are only a pair of boots, Rachel," he responded. "I know you have trouble taking stuff, but I want to thank you."

He rested his hand on the roof of her car. "I know you don't like owing people anything. I already figured out that much about you. I'm the same. The boots and the ride are my way of balancing the scales."

She seemed to understand that. She relaxed, a bit, and

buckled the child into her car seat then climbed into the driver's side.

Travis folded himself into the passenger seat. Rachel, looking thoughtful, switched on the radio before backing out of the driveway.

At the Double U, they found both Udall and Uma in their front yard, Uma as compact and weathered as her husband.

"You mind if I take Dusty out in a corral to give Tori a ride?"

Uma grinned, sending one set of wrinkles on a collision course with another. "Of course not. Make yourselves at home. Hey, Rachel, how's the pregnancy going?"

"This baby can't come soon enough." Despite the sentiment, Rachel laughed.

A man would never tire of that laugh.

Travis took them to the stable and introduced them to Dusty.

Tori grasped his pant leg at the knee and sidled against him. "He's big, Travis."

Dusty wasn't some cute pony from a book. Travis picked her up. "Not when you're way up high like this. That better?"

She nodded, but still looked trepidatious, if that was a word.

"Here." Uma's arm appeared from behind him holding a carrot. "Give him this."

Tori took it and held it out in her tiny hand. Dusty, perhaps sensing how scared she was, took it as gently as Travis had ever seen.

"His chewing is loud." Tori seemed to be coming around.

Travis turned to Rachel. "Take her outside, and I'll saddle Dusty and bring him out through the far doors to the corral. I'll get in the saddle, and you hand her to me, okay?"

Once Dusty was ready to go, Travis walked him out and mounted.

Tori sat on top of the fence, with Uma keeping her steady. Travis reached down and took her into his arms, turning her to face forward. He locked his arm across her small waist and scooted her back against him so she'd feel safe, those ridiculous miniature pink cowboy boots sticking out from her splayed legs.

"Okay? You ready to ride, Little Miss Cowgirl?"

She giggled. "Yeah. Just a bit, Travis. Not fast, 'kay?"

"You got it." He urged Dusty into the most sedate walk imaginable. The horse looked back over his shoulder as if to ask what the heck was going on.

"Easy, Dusty, we got precious cargo." Dusty plodded around the corral.

Tori clapped her hands. "Mommy, look, I'm riding a horse. I'm a cowgirl!"

When Travis glanced at Rachel, her full-fledged happiness knocked his socks off. Her eyes looked suspiciously damp. *Thank you*, she mouthed. Apparently, anything was all right with her as long as it made her daughter happy.

He smiled back because this was one spectacular ride. He and Dusty loved to burn up the prairie, loved to ride to race the wind, but even his horse seemed to sense how important this moment was.

The happy bundle in his arms and the grateful woman on the other side of the fence sent his pleasure through the stratosphere.

God, he'd been lonely.

LATE THAT NIGHT, Travis had no idea why he couldn't sleep. His shoulders and biceps ached from the renovations he'd started today after returning Tori and Rachel to their trailer. He should be exhausted from washing the walls and prepping them to be painted. He was, but damned if he could get to sleep.

No sense lying in bed, staring at the ceiling. He got up and went downstairs.

He'd seen the white cat hanging around the front yard. Poor creature was going to get herself killed if she wasn't careful. He wondered what she was living on. Field mice?

In the kitchen, he opened a tin of tuna and put it on one of the saucers from the old set of dishes he'd found in the cabinets he'd scrubbed down today. He grabbed a cold beer from the fridge and the bag of licorice whips he'd picked up at the general store and headed for the front porch.

Snagging a thick, fleece-lined flannel jacket, he donned it before sitting on the veranda steps. He deposited the tuna at the foot of the stairs. Quietly he waited, taking an occasional sip from the bottle and chewing on licorice.

Eventually, Ghost appeared, as pale in the moonlight as her namesake. She sniffed the tuna. With a low growl, she tucked in.

The rough sputter of an engine approached and the Focus pulled into Cindy's driveway. Home from work, Rachel stepped out with her purse and a thermal lunch bag.

She glanced around, doing a double take when she noticed him sitting on the steps and Ghost eating at his feet.

She crossed the road and walked up his driveway. "How'd you get her to come out?"

"I opened a tin of tuna."

The blond highlights in her caramel hair shone in the dim moonlight. "Her favorite," she said. "Abigail used to feed it to her instead of cat food."

"It was the only thing I could think to give her. Got lucky, I guess."

"You sure did."

Travis held out the bag of licorice. "Whip?"

"Red! My favorite."

His, too. She took one and bit into it. He scooted over so she could sit down.

"How was work?" he asked, voice low and soft. Not that he would wake anyone out here in the back of beyond, but it seemed a shame to disturb the peaceful night.

"Busy! Whew." Rachel whuffed out a breath of air that stirred wisps of hair. "You'd think the state was about to put a ban on beer. Honey's was packed."

"Good for tips."

"Yeah," she said, her voice as quiet as his own. "Good for tips."

Suddenly, she leaned forward and peered at the saucer Ghost was licking clean. She yelped. "You used Abigail's Royal Doulton for the *cat*?"

"Her what?"

"Her Lady Carlisle china?"

Lady *who*? He shrugged. It was a saucer with flowers on it. "So what?"

"So…it's worth a fortune. It's one of the prettiest patterns ever made."

It was too fussy for him. "I've got a whole set inside."

Rachel pressed a hand to her chest, drawing his eyes to her round bosom. Hard to tell what her natural bust would look like. Must be bigger than usual because of the baby. He shook his head. Why was he thinking about that? Why was he even looking?

"You've got the whole set?" She sounded breathless.

"Yep. It came with the house."

"Don't ever throw it out or give it away. Ever. I'll save from now until Doomsday and buy it from you."

"Okay. I need to use it for now, though. I have nothing else. I'll buy a plastic bowl for the cat."

After that, they said nothing, just chewed on their licorice and watched Ghost.

Rachel's silence was restful. From the moment his sister became a teenager, Samantha had started to talk nonstop, big on air and slim on depth. She could talk the ears off a field of corn. Travis loved his sister, but it bordered on too much.

Finished with her meal, Ghost mounted the steps and sat beside Travis to lick her paws.

"You've made a conquest." Humor hummed in Rachel's voice. "All these months I've been trying to feed her, I made the mistake of buying *cat* food instead of people food. What *was* I thinking?"

Travis chuckled. For a while, they settled into silence, and he felt himself relax, Rachel being an easy woman to spend time with.

Sammy and the boys would do well here. They would be safe. No worries.

His curiosity got the better of him, and he broke the silence.

"Why is this house so important to you?"

He sensed her stiffen beside him. Damn. He hadn't meant to make her uncomfortable.

"I…um…didn't always have the happiest childhood." A sigh that sounded like it came up from the soles of her worn cowboy boots gusted out of her. "My mom and my grandparents fought a lot."

"Why?"

"They were all the same. Stubborn. Not one of them would ever give an inch." She squeezed one hand inside the other. "Mostly, it was about me. My mom had me when she was only fifteen. Her parents never let her live it down."

"And your dad?"

"Gone before I was born. I never knew him."

"I'm sorry." He knew it wasn't enough, but he wasn't used to giving solace. Didn't know how.

She shrugged. "I've learned to live with it."

Sounded to Travis like maybe she still carried that loss inside her.

"The trailer is small. Even with only four of us, it felt crowded. When the fighting got bad," she went on, "I would come over here to visit Abigail. She was sweet and loving. She would make me tea and homemade cookies. Only time in my life I had homemade baked goods."

At least she had some good memories.

"I grew to love the house as well as Abigail. It was big, without a bunch of people crammed into two bedrooms in a trailer surrounded by dirt. It was always calm here. I loved the romance of the refined Victorian design on the rugged prairie."

They were quiet for a while, settling back into the earlier easiness.

Finally, she said, "It's time for me to head home. Thanks again for your help today with the car, and for taking Tori out on your horse. She was still chattering about it when I left for work."

Good. Favors and gifts balanced and reciprocated. He'd given her something in return for that magical carousel ride.

With the scales balanced and the slate wiped clean, he owed no one a single thing.

She stood to leave. "You've made yourself a friend in Ghost. Enjoy."

"Good night," he said, while the cat deigned to allow him to pet her.

Travis watched Rachel take her time crossing to her own house with the slightest waddle. Not a pretty term, but that's what it was. What was most surprising to Travis was that he'd never noticed before that a pregnant woman's walk could be so feminine.

For several minutes after Rachel silently entered her own house, Travis remained on his dark porch, running his fingers along Ghost's knobby spine, pondering woman-hood and the many attractive forms it could take.

"She's home," he whispered to the purring cat. "Safe."

Travis picked up the Royal Lady Somebody china saucer and entered his house, thinking that he'd better head into town tomorrow to pick up a flea collar for the cat. He had the feeling they were going to be buddies, but no way was she bringing pests into the house he was getting ready for his boys. He closed the door behind himself, leaving the cat outside complaining.

He lay on his bed and, moments later, the nervous energy that had dogged him earlier was history…and that was a bad sign.

Sure, through years of ingrained habit, he was used to helping women who needed help, but this thing with Rachel, whatever it was, was dangerous.

He didn't want her making him feel better about himself. He didn't want her making him feel restful instead of restless.

He didn't want to be lured, seduced, lulled into taking on more than he wanted in life.

Starting tomorrow morning, he would guard his heart better and keep his distance.

He owed the woman nothing.

SUNDAY MORNING FOUND Rachel behind the back of the trailer clearing out the rest of the old plants she hadn't managed to finish pulling from the garden yesterday.

It should have been done in late September. With November breathing down her neck, Rachel still hadn't finished.

Tori sat at the small plastic picnic table Rachel had bought for her that summer. She drew pictures of animals and colored them in, currently working on a purple-and-black tiger. Or what she said was a tiger. It looked like a blob on legs with stripes, sort of like Rachel herself these days. Without the stripes.

Despite the coolness of the day, she wiped sweat from her forehead with her sleeve.

Cindy came out of the house with a jug of iced tea and three plastic glasses.

"You going to finish cleaning out your vegetable garden today?"

"I should be able to, yes."

"Why?" Cindy put the items she carried onto Tori's table. "We can buy all the vegetables we want from the grocery store."

"I know, but I like organic and can't afford to buy it, so I grow veggies. Besides, the cost is a lot cheaper than even the regular vegetables at the store."

Rachel raked out the portion of the garden she'd already cleared. Economizing was important to her. She paid Cindy rent and bought all of the groceries for herself and Tori. No one, least of all her mother, could ever accuse her of being a freeloader.

And then there were those boxes of Mason jars hidden in her closet into which she put every penny she could spare.

"It's a lot of work, Rachel. You should be keeping the weight off your feet today. Relax. Take care of that baby."

"The baby's fine." Sometimes she got tired of people fussing about the baby. For once, she would like people to see her, just her, and not her pregnant belly. Like Travis often did, looking past the baby to her.

Oh, stop that, Rachel. He sees your pregnant belly as much as anyone does. Doesn't he?

"If we want vegetables planted come spring," she said, "I need to get this year's plants out. I can't leave them to rot over the winter."

With another mouth to feed, next year's garden would

be even more essential. She planned to make her own baby food for Beth, just as she had for Tori.

"It's your funeral." Cindy filled a plastic tumbler with iced tea. "Here, have some of this while I finish up."

"No, Cindy, it's my job." It was a matter of pride that Rachel should pull her own weight.

"Sit. Drink." She handed Tori a smidgen of tea.

Cindy grabbed the rake from Rachel, who hung on, and they grappled for it.

"Oh, for God's sake," Rachel said. The two of them let go at the same time and ended up on their backsides in the garden.

Tori pointed and giggled. "Funny!"

Cindy picked up a handful of leaves Rachel had already raked together and tossed them at her daughter. Rachel threw a bunch back. Tori joined in, and it turned into a glorious free-for-all.

They ended up lying on their backs on the grass staring at clouds scudding across a blue sky, spent from laughing hard.

It brought back memories of when Rachel was small and Cindy still so young she used to sit on the floor and play with her daughter as though she were her friend instead of her mother. They'd loved dressing dolls together.

"Is the baby okay?" Cindy asked.

Lazily, Rachel nodded. "She's fine. I'm pregnant, not sick." Even so, she reached out and squeezed her mother's hand. It was nice for Cindy to actually *be* motherly.

Cindy stood and picked up the rake. "Even if I don't agree with all the work you put into this, I'm not the Wicked Witch of the West, you know."

Rachel sat up and took a sip of tea. She hid a smile behind her plastic cup. Yeah, some days Mom was the Wicked Witch of the West, but not today, and it was nice to work beside her in harmony.

After Rachel finished her drink, she carried two bags of yard waste out to the curb for pickup in the morning.

The Victorian caught her eye, as it always did.

The house with its cockeyed periwinkle-blue shutters, gap-toothed white gingerbread scrollwork and wraparound veranda basked in the Montana sunshine like a forgotten wedding cake.

Overdone and civilized amid the simple wild splendor of the valley in the shadow of the distant Tendoy Mountains, it was a house only a lonely girl would fantasize about. Rachel loved every overly decorated inch of it.

Her phone rang. She pulled it out of her pocket.

"Hey, Rachel." Nadine's voice drifted over the airwaves.

"Nadine, what's up?"

"I investigated him just like you asked me to."

"What? Who?"

An exasperated sigh filled the line. "Travis Read."

Rachel had forgotten. In her disappointment on Friday, she had asked Nadine to dig up dirt. Now she regretted that rash decision.

"You work quickly," she told her friend.

"With the internet, it's a heck of a lot easier to find things than it used to be."

"What did you learn?" While she waited for Nadine's response, Rachel held her breath. She liked Travis. She really liked him. She didn't want dirt. She didn't want to know his secrets.

"Surprisingly, there isn't that much to tell outside of the man being a wanderer. He sure does move around a lot, every year as far as I can tell. He's had a lot of different addresses in the past ten years."

Rachel's heart sank. She had been fathered by a drifter. Cindy's dating life had been littered with them.

After Rachel had been raised without a dad, she'd vowed to never do that to her kids. Then she'd fallen for a guy who had died too young through his own foolishness, and her children were left without a father after all.

The only man she needed was one who was dependable, reliable and who would love Rodeo as much as she did. A man who wouldn't mock her town as some of those drifters passing through had or who wouldn't laugh at how hard she worked to get that old amusement park up and running again to save this town. She needed someone who would stick around.

Not that it mattered. No man would be interested in her. She came with too much baggage even for the most dependable man.

She had no one to lean on but herself.

"Thanks, Nadine," she murmured.

"Anytime, hon. Take care of yourself. Remind me when you're due?"

"First week of December."

"Let's get together before then."

"You bet."

She ended the call and sat on the porch step, shaken. Travis Read might be a decent guy, but he was a wanderer.

She stared at the beautiful Victorian that had been a beacon of safety all of her life.

He'd bought the house for his sister and nephews, not for himself. She'd known that but had assumed he would be staying there, too.

She'd been a fool to let him get under her skin. She had also been a daydreaming fool to think that last night's quiet, friendly conversation meant anything.

Terrifically awful premature flickers of feeling had developed in her and kept her awake last night.

She would have to guard her heart with a ruthless hand.

Even aware of the differences in their situations, she had dreamed anyway, so unwisely.

Already, she'd fallen far enough into a bad state of infatuation when nothing would ever be returned. Worse, the man would probably be moving on soon after his sister arrived.

Rachel might be a daydreamer, but she was *not* her mother, falling for one dissatisfied wanderer after another.

She pulled herself under control. *No more dreaming. Face reality, Rachel. Accept it and live with it.*

At least there might be someone for Tori to play with in that house. After all, her children's happiness was more important than hers. Just once, though, she would like a little something for herself.

Rachel tugged on the hem of Davey's old, fraying sweatshirt and stood. *No self-pity, Rachel. It's a waste of time.*

"Mommy, can we play in the leaves again?"

Yep. Tori was more important. How could a woman possibly feel sorry for herself when she had an amazing child to spend time with? So what if Tori wasn't a man who could offer support and warm arms, filling her with affection and sating her yearning body?

That would have to wait until after she'd finished with the responsibilities she'd taken on with wide-open eyes.

ON SUNDAY MORNING, Travis headed into town for breakfast again.

He wanted to get to know more of the townsfolk. He managed to snag a stool at the counter beside Cole Payette.

They had a good conversation about everything ranging from ranching, to next year's rodeo, to their favorite sports teams.

Cole filled him in on plenty of details about Rodeo. Seemed like Travis had done well in choosing this town for Samantha.

They chatted through breakfast, and Travis came away with a positive impression of Cole.

Good. Travis just might need the man on his side if

Manny D'Onofrio ever found out where Samantha ended up. Not that he would. Travis had been ultra-careful.

Even so, Sammy's former boss in Las Vegas was a man of means who fostered a dangerous loyalty in his more fanatical employees. Who knew what that might mean if Manny located Sammy?

He filled Cole in on some of the details of Manny's trial for embezzlement. Sammy, who'd worked briefly as an accountant for Manny, had blown the whistle on him and had testified in court. Manny held a grudge.

Hence, Travis's need to get Sammy settled out here in the back of beyond using her own name instead of her husband's.

As sheriff, Cole needed to know.

After breakfast, Travis drove out to the big mall on the main highway to get pet supplies because the stores in town were closed on Sunday. Along with a flea collar, he also bought a plastic bowl and a cat brush to get the mats out of Ghost's fur.

Back home, he slowed to turn into his driveway.

Rachel and Tori stood in theirs.

Before he caught himself with his new resolve to stay aloof, he waved.

The little one smiled and waved back, but Rachel offered only a brisk nod.

He got out of the truck with his purchases and walked across the road.

Rachel didn't smile, didn't wave, didn't greet him with anything remotely akin to her normal goodwill.

Something had changed this morning.

"What's that?" Tori pointed to the pet-store bag.

Yesterday, he and Rachel had been friends. Last night, they'd spent precious moments sitting on his veranda in a state of harmony he'd never felt before.

Friendship with a woman other than his sister had been as foreign in his life as carousel rides and boyhood dreams.

Sure, he'd decided to keep his distance, but what had changed in Rachel since last night?

An iceberg separated them. He didn't have a clue why.

He answered the child's question. "A flea collar for Ghost."

"Look, Travis. I'm wearing my new boots."

"I can see that. They sure do look good on you." Knowing how much her child's happiness mattered to Rachel, he glanced at her. Once again, her gaze flitted away. No smile. No shared enjoyment of Tori's joy in a flimsy pair of boots.

Nothing. Nada.

Awkwardness settled over him.

She turned and directed her daughter into the trailer without saying goodbye.

Travis shook his head, at sea.

Only a couple of days after meeting the woman, he cared about the potential friendship that had seemed to be building between them.

He walked to his own place, but stopped on the veranda to glance back.

Sure, he'd recognized the danger in finding her so appealing, but he'd had it under control. He'd flat out just liked talking to her. That's all. Just talking. Just relaxing with a friend.

Now that was gone.

The distance between their homes might be only a few yards, but the distance between their hearts was a whole universe long.

Chapter Seven

Throughout his first week on the ranch, Travis worked hard. He'd never been a slacker, but making a good impression on Udall and Uma seemed to be more important to him than with any other employer.

He liked them. He liked the town.

He wanted his family to fit in after he left.

In return, he wanted to be respected, to be the kind of man his father had never been.

It seemed that, at the ripe old age of thirty-seven, he was growing into himself and becoming his own man.

All it had taken was his sister's crisis for him to realize how fragile life was, and how fleeting peace could be.

The first couple of days, all he did was chase down cattle hidden in the most remote, thorniest spots, riding through the roughest terrain on the ranch.

"They always pick the worst spots to hunker down in," he commented to Udall after they'd found yet another one grazing on the side of a small mountain. "That isn't even the sweetest grass on the prairie."

"Ain't that the truth? Don't know why." Udall turned his horse toward the hill. "Let's get him."

Twenty minutes later, they'd routed the animal and trailed him back toward home.

Day after day, Travis rode the Weber ranch, getting to know its contours, its beauties and its tough spots.

When he was out on his own, he radioed one of the hands, Bill Young, with observations about broken fence lines and whatever else needed attention.

Bill would come along later on an ATV, what most cowboys called a Japanese quarter horse, and mend as needed.

In the evenings, even as he had a hasty dinner and stripped woodwork, he kept half an eye on the trailer across the road.

Unsettled by his last encounter with Rachel, and her cool reaction to him, he had an urge to see her, to find out what had happened. What had he done to offend her?

His chance came on Thursday night. Already tired of his own cooking, he headed into Honey's Place for a beer and burger.

He showered, shaved, donned fresh jeans and a clean shirt and headed back out.

Rachel was at the bar filling an order.

The place wasn't as packed as it had been last Friday night, but a good crowd filled probably two-thirds of the tables.

He searched for a table near where he'd sat with Cindy last week, hoping it would be in Rachel's serving area.

When she approached, he knew he'd hit the jackpot.

She didn't return his smile. He'd expected that.

Until he sorted out what the problem was, he figured he'd get more of the same treatment. How to approach her, though?

"Hey," he said.

"What can I get for you?" she asked. He guessed she had to be polite. He was a customer. She had no choice.

He decided to test her. "Same order as last week."

"Okay," she said and walked away with the unopened menu and no questions asked.

She returned with a Corona.

Fifteen minutes later, out came his dinner, a perfect

replica of last week's meal. She'd remembered. She was one hell of a good waitress.

She set the burger and onion rings on the table in front of him without making eye contact.

"Rachel," he said.

She added the plate of hot wings.

"Rachel, please."

She put down his coleslaw and made to leave, but he grasped her wrist. He could feel a fine tremor beneath his palm.

"Tell me what I did wrong."

"Nothing. Everything's fine."

"It isn't and we both know it. I just can't figure what I did."

At last she looked at him. What he saw in her eyes puzzled him. She wasn't angry, but hurt. He recognized more of that quiet acceptance of less that he'd seen when her car broke down.

What did that attitude have to do with him?

How was he asking her to expect less from him? He'd never offered her anything, so how could she expect little?

"What did I do?"

Her pulse beat rapidly against his fingers. "You did nothing wrong."

"Then what changed? On Saturday night, we were almost friends. On Sunday morning, you were treating me like an enemy."

"I wasn't." Her eyes flashed.

"Okay. Maybe not that badly. But you were warm and friendly until then. Since then, you've been cold."

Talking so much, delving into problems, was out of character for him, but he wanted to know.

His eyes dropped to her belly. The last thing he needed was a ready-made family. So maybe it was best that things were rough between them. Why did he care?

The answer hit him in the solar plexus. He *liked* her. It wasn't a case of wanting to take her to bed, though under different circumstances, he would sleep with her in a heartbeat.

The important thing here was that he just plain *liked* her...and had enjoyed her high regard of him.

It hurt that he'd lost her respect.

If he couldn't get it back, so be it, but he at least wanted to understand why.

He squeezed her wrist gently, noting that she hadn't pulled her hand away. She could have. He would have let go at the least resistance.

"Tell me what happened."

She relented, eased that rigid backbone a fraction, and signaled to Honey she was sitting down for a minute.

RACHEL WASN'T A COWARD, but tonight she felt like one, for one simple reason. Embarrassment.

She didn't want to tell Travis that she'd spied on him.

How was she supposed to explain that she didn't want him to be a drifter when that fact shouldn't affect her at all?

She peeked at him. He watched her steadily.

She counted herself a good judge of character, mainly because of the revolving door of Cindy's love life. She'd learned a lot growing up in Cindy's trailer, strictly by virtue of watching, listening and keeping her mouth shut.

Beyond a shadow of a doubt, Travis was a good guy.

Too bad he liked to move around.

Again, that had nothing to do with her.

First to break the silence, he said, "What's up, Rachel?"

She ran a fingernail along the seam of the wooden table. What could she say? *I'm attracted to you? I like you? I'm pregnant and already a mother, but I want a relationship with you? And why shouldn't you want to leave when you hear that?*

Might as well get this thing started. "I might have asked my friend Nadine at the newspaper to check you out."

"Check me out? Why?" A frown furrowed his brow. He wasn't happy about this. If the tables were turned, she wouldn't be, either.

"You just seemed too perfect. I was angry that you'd bought the house. I wanted to find a reason to dislike you."

He perked up. "You thought I was perfect?"

She sent him a lowering look. "Maybe. Anyway, that was last Friday. I forgot I'd asked her. I really didn't want to spy. I was just upset that the house was sold to someone else."

"So? Why the cold shoulder?"

"Nadine called on Sunday."

"And?" He moved his hand in a circular motion, urging her on.

"And she said you never stay in the same place for more than a year."

He was silent for so long she wondered what he was thinking. She glanced up. He watched her without flinching, his expression shuttered.

"Why would that make you angry?" When she didn't respond, he continued, "Why would you be angry with a guy you've known only a week just because he might leave town next year?"

She chose her words carefully. Crushes were for teenage girls, not grown women with children. It was too, too embarrassing to admit to Travis that she *liked* him, especially so quickly.

Suppressing memories of that incredible kiss they'd shared when he was injured on the highway, she forced herself to deal in generalities.

"First, let me apologize for being cold. It was an unreasonable response."

She gathered her thoughts.

"Cindy's had an endless string of boyfriends, mostly men passing through because she's already dated all the eligible men in town. And some who were ineligible. Nothing good has ever come of those relationships."

She motioned for him to eat. No sense in letting all of that good food to go to waste. "It was hard to grow up with that, seeing all of those men use my mom and then leave town. Cindy has her faults, but she doesn't deserve to be treated so callously."

"No, she doesn't. She has a good heart even if she is too needy."

"Yeah, that's the right word."

"So you think I might use Cindy and then leave?"

She hadn't given Cindy a single thought.

"No. It's just that I've developed a dislike of drifters."

His spine stiffened. "I'm not a drifter. Yeah, I move on after a while, but I don't take advantage of others. I earn my own keep. I'm a hard worker."

"Dear Lord, I know that, Travis. I can see that. All you do every night is work on that house, and that's after putting in a day of hard work for Udall."

A tiny smile kicked up the corners of his mouth. Her gaze darted away because it set her nerves humming. "You've been talking to Udall about me?"

"No!" Okay, maybe she had run across Uma in the grocery store and had possibly asked her how Travis was doing on the ranch, to which Uma had responded with a resounding, "Boy, that man can work!" But she'd hadn't talked to Udall, so she wasn't lying, was she?

"My response to what Nadine told me wasn't logical, Travis. It was emotional. I've seen too many men come and go over the years for me to trust a traveler."

"What does that have to do with me?"

Dear Lord, don't let him guess how much I care already, she prayed.

"It's just my response to all new people in town."

He nodded.

"I'm not a drifter, Rachel," he stated emphatically, again, as though that were all she needed to know.

Thank goodness Travis didn't bring up how friendly she'd been on his first morning in town, giving him a ride on the carousel and all.

Her aim was to get out of this discussion in one piece without plopping her heart out on the table like a sacrifice.

A family came in for dinner, and that ended the conversation. Rachel stood to welcome them and take their orders. She'd managed to keep it general. Travis would never suspect how much she liked him, and how much she wanted him to be the staying kind.

She walked away knowing she hadn't gained anything from the conversation. She hadn't heard the only thing she'd wanted to, the most *unreasonable*, improbable, impossible thing she could ever wish for.

He hadn't said, "I would stay for you."

McGuire, you are such a daydreamer.

Travis was still awake hours later, going over his conversation with Rachel. He was glad they'd talked, but still didn't understand why his comings and goings mattered to her.

He wasn't about to become involved with Cindy, so what difference did it make if he left in a year, or less?

He heard a car turn into her driveway across the road and glanced out the window, but it wasn't Rachel's car.

He threw on a coat and stepped outside.

Rachel approached her door as a car driven by Honey backed out of the driveway and took off.

"What happened to your car?" He didn't need to raise his voice. In the stillness of the night, she would hear him. He walked down his driveway.

Rachel turned. "It wouldn't start."

"Again?" He crossed the road. "Want me to go boost it for you?"

"Not at this time of night. You need to get up early. Why are you still up?"

He wouldn't tell her the truth. *Because our talk kept me awake. Because I still can't figure out why it matters to you if I stay or go, or why your opinion of me matters to me.*

"Couldn't sleep," was all he admitted to. "Let's go start your car."

Cripes, Travis, what are you doing? You've got a whole shitload of crazy going on right now. You do not need to help this woman.

"Tomorrow's Friday. Mom takes Tori to the mall for their girl-bonding. I'll get into town somehow and get the car started then."

"Let's do it now."

"Why are you pushing this so hard?"

"I need…"

"You need?"

"To know you're safe. That you can get around tomorrow if you need to. That you have a working vehicle."

"Travis, I'm not your responsibility."

"I know." Even to his own ears, he sounded confused. "Please get in the truck and let's get this done."

"Okay," she said, but looked as puzzled as he felt.

The second they were both buckled in, she started to talk, all about independence and going her own way and being a capable woman, thank you very much. She didn't need any man to take care of her. She was fine on her own.

And yet, here she was in his truck.

He figured she could give him a piece of her mind all she wanted. It beat the hell out of the silent treatment she'd given him this past week. He didn't ever want to be on the receiving end of that again.

When she wound down a mile shy of town, he said, "Rachel, I know you're capable." To his surprise, he realized he meant it. He worried about her when he shouldn't. Her business was her own.

He scrubbed the back of his neck.

"You're right," he said, and meant it. "You are independent. You're doing a great job with your daughter. You did a great job with the carousel. You are a kick-ass waitress. The townspeople love and respect you."

Next, he said something he'd never found easy. "I'm sorry."

She took her time, but eventually nodded. "Thanks. I appreciate the apology."

A moment later, she asked, "What was it for?"

"I've been high-handed at times."

He sensed her nodding beside him.

"Know what I need from you?"

He'd piqued her curiosity. He felt her watching him.

"No, what?"

"I need a friend. You're the best person I've met in this town. We both know I'll be leaving at some point. I have no designs on your mother, so she won't get hurt. You've got a whole barrel of responsibilities that have nothing to do with me, and you're independent as you said, so you won't be demanding a lot of me."

Whew, an entire speech. What was it about this woman that had him opening up and talking so much?

Something in the honest, straightforward way she dealt with people demanded no less from him.

"You want me to be your friend?"

She seemed a mite disappointed. He didn't know why.

To his mind, friendship was the best gift a person could offer. It was worth all the gems in the world.

"Yeah. I didn't like when you weren't talking to me."

There he went spilling his beans again.

"It hurt when you were cold."

His admission seemed to please her.

"Okay. We can be friends."

"Okay, then. Don't friends help each other out in times of need?"

"Yes."

"And this is a time of need."

"For me, yes. Here's the problem, though." She shifted in her seat. "When will there ever be a time for me to give something back to you?"

He cast a startled glance at her. "You don't know?"

"Know what?"

"The carousel ride, to start."

"You already paid me back for that."

"I know. I guess I can't stress enough how huge it was. Sammy and me—"

He could feel her eyes on him.

"Sammy and you?"

"We didn't have anything. Dad drank too much and Mom was…" He shrugged, trying to minimize what they'd gone through. He wasn't looking for pity. "Best way I can describe her is weak. She wasn't a bad person, but she didn't have a lot to give. Sammy and I were on our own. Then they died."

She rubbed one hand on her thigh. "I'm sorry."

"I don't want you to feel sorry for me. I just want you to understand how it was. We had nothing. No money. No stuff. I kept us together by working every waking hour I wasn't going to school. After Mom died, I had to drop out."

They arrived in front of Honey's. He pulled up beside Rachel's car.

"There were no extras, no movies, no county fairs, no music. That ride you gave me was…" He had to stop talking because he'd become emotional. He wasn't an emotional man.

A moment later, he cleared his throat. "When I was growing up, there was no joy." He turned in his seat to face her, desperate for her to understand. "You gave me joy."

Her whiskey eyes looked suspiciously moist. She tucked a strand of tawny hair behind her ear. One silver cowboy-boot earring winked at him in the dim light from Honey's front door.

"Travis, that's the best thing anyone's ever said to me."

"There's more. When I felt your baby talking to me…" When her eyes widened, he amended, "I mean when I felt her moving, it was like she was communicating with me. Acknowledging me, or something. Strange, huh?"

"No, not strange. I feel the same way. Sometimes when she moves, it feels like she's playing with me already."

"You've given me two gifts the likes of which I could never repay. My point is that you have to understand why I need to help you out when I can. Okay?"

"Okay. Just be less bossy about it."

"I can do that."

They got out of the truck. Rachel sat in the driver's seat of her car.

Travis boosted the battery, closed her hood and came around to her open driver's window. "Consider scraping together enough cash to get yourself another cheap clunker. There's got to be a better one out there."

"I'll think about it." She smiled, not one of her dazzlers, but a quiet, thoughtful one. He found it no less attractive than the bright, shiny ones.

"Thank you, Travis. Thanks for explaining things to me."

The wind picked up, and he tamped his hat more firmly onto his head. "I'm a lot more than just a macho dude, you know."

"A bossy macho dude."

"I'll try to do better."

"Promises, promises."

Chapter Eight

Weekdays, Travis spent long hours on the ranch, collecting cattle and mending fence before the snows set in.

Weeknights, he'd spend longer evenings working on the house, getting it ready for his sister and her boys.

Sometime before Christmas, they would be driving in from San Francisco. He didn't want them here while he renovated. He wanted to give them a perfect house.

Friday and Saturday nights became a pleasure for him, a break away from the endless work. He'd spend them at Honey's, getting to know his neighbors and dancing up a storm.

That Rachel worked there was an added bonus he didn't look at too closely.

Cole Payette was becoming a good buddy. More often than not, Travis found himself on a stool beside Cole at the bar getting to know the man better. Saturday mornings found him having breakfast with the guy on stools at the counter in Vy's diner.

It might seem like they had little in common, Cole being a one-town man and Travis a nomad, but they never lacked for conversation. And their quiet moments were companionable.

It had been a long time since Travis had had a good friend, someone closer than a mere acquaintance.

When he arrived home after a night out, he would say,

"Come on, Ghost," and walk into the house, followed by the newly clean cat.

As it got colder, Ghost took to spending more time inside than out.

She became a permanent resident and his new companion. He sure hoped Sammy wouldn't mind keeping the cat.

"Who would have thought," he murmured to her one night, "that I'd take on not only a house, but also a pet."

He shook his head and kept on stripping the floors. Later, while enjoying a beer in front of the fire, Ghost jumped onto the sofa and curled up beside him. He liked the feel of her warm weight against his leg.

In mid-November, the town held a Thanksgiving dance in the elementary school auditorium.

Brown, orange and red construction paper leaves covered the walls along with the obligatory rows of hooks for cowboy hats. He'd come to learn the town took its hat hooks seriously.

Good thing, since Travis took *his* hat seriously.

In the middle of the evening, five women took to the stage.

Rachel stood in the middle, with Honey to her right and Violet from the diner to her left. Standing beside Travis, Cole leaned close and identified the other two for him.

"Nadine and Max. The official park committee. They're the ones who've spearheaded the revival of the amusement park."

"Think they'll get it done on time?"

Cole grinned. "No doubt in my mind at all. They're driven."

They were an attractive bunch, all in their late twenties. Honey wore her trademark turquoise and silver jewelry. Her mass of blond hair hung in curls to her waist.

Violet wore her distinctive forties and fifties retro style. In the diner, she pinned her hair up beneath a kerchief, but tonight her straight blue-black hair hung down her back in striking contrast to her violet eyes.

Nadine had beautiful red hair every bit as straight as Vy's.

The last woman on stage, Max, stood out by how boyish she looked compared to the other women—Rachel womanly in her pregnancy, and Honey with her masses of curls, Vy with her hourglass figure and Nadine with her perfect manicure, makeup and sparkly party dress.

Max wore a boxy plaid shirt, torn jeans and broken-in cowboy boots.

"Folks," Rachel began, "you all know who we are and why we're here tonight. We're the reason you paid for tickets to the Thanksgiving dance for the first time ever."

Her microphone squealed, and someone adjusted the sound.

"I love this town," she continued with an emphasis on *love*. "I don't want it to die. Our young people are leaving in droves. If we get the rides fixed and offer great deals on unique entertainment, we can bring in tourists. We'll top it off with a first-rate rodeo. Our goal is to open for three weeks next August and later expand into something that will last longer."

Her passion for the project shone through, and Travis saw a glimpse of the woman he'd met on his first morning in town.

The world would be a pretty awesome place if all of Rachel McGuire's burdens could be eased and this Rachel could be present all the time. She was magnetic.

"We thank you all for your generosity," Honey said. "Many of you bought more than one ticket, and it's appreciated. The money will go a long way toward revitalizing both the amusement park and our town."

Travis heard something that sounded like a sigh from Cole, who stared at Honey. He nudged him with his shoulder.

"How many did you buy?" Travis asked.

"Only ten."

"Only?"

Cole shrugged. His cheeks turned suspiciously pink.

"Let it go, Read."

"Sure thing, Payette."

A moment later, Cole asked, "How many did you buy?"

"Only a dozen."

The corners of Cole's mouth kicked up. "Only?"

"Let it go, Payette."

"Sure thing, Read."

They stood in companionable silence throughout the speeches.

When they ended and music started up for dancing, Travis sought out Rachel.

"Tell me about the women you've teamed up with to resurrect the fair."

"You know Honey. She'll be in charge of entertainment."

"She'd be good at that." Travis grinned. "What will Vy be doing?"

"Food."

"Makes sense."

"And Nadine? I haven't met her. What will she be doing?"

"Promotion and hospitality."

"And last, the one on the far end. What was her name?"

"Maxine Porter. Max. She'll resurrect the rodeo that started it all and gave the town its name."

"Sounds like you have everything covered."

"I think so. We'll have to work hard, but we're all up for it."

Rachel glanced around the room.

"I love this place and these people." She turned her gaze to him, her eyes luminous and sad. "I couldn't possibly ever leave. I love my friends. I want my children to grow up here. My own childhood might not have been ideal, but the town is. It's worth preserving."

"What is it, Rachel? Why so sad?"

"I feel like this is our last chance. What if we can't make this happen? What if tourists don't come? There's nothing else here. No industry. No manufacturing. The ranching is good, but it can't keep the whole town afloat. Beef prices rise and rise and people eat less and less of it."

Someone bumped into them, and Travis pulled her close. They ended up slow dancing with the flow of the crowd.

"I'm afraid we might fail. Then where will the town be?"

"Why wouldn't you succeed?" he asked.

She shook her head, clearly suffering a lack of confidence. First time he'd seen that in her.

"Know what I saw when I watched you five women on stage?"

"No. What?"

"A smart, determined group of women. Starting with you."

"Really? Starting with me?"

"Yeah."

They stopped speaking and stopped moving. The air around them seemed to become rarefied. The coconut scent of her shampoo drifted around them. While Rachel turned her brilliant golden eyes on him, Travis lost the ability to breathe, let alone think or talk.

Move, Travis. This isn't what you want. Friendship, remember? Only friendship.

The song changed, but Rachel stayed in his arms until a moment later when she gasped, breaking the spell.

Travis followed the direction of her gaze. Cindy was dancing with a man Travis didn't recognize.

"Who's that?" he asked.

"A stranger. He was in the bar the other night asking about job prospects in town."

Travis studied her keenly. "You didn't like him." He didn't need her to answer. He sensed the tension in her.

"I thought he was less than honest. He bragged about all the places he'd been."

"Ah, I see."

"What does that mean?"

"The man's a drifter. That's an automatic strike against him."

"That was some of it." He liked her unflinching honesty, even about herself. "Not all, though. It was more than a knee-jerk reaction on my part. I don't know what his game is. The only thing I feel for certain is that there is a game."

Travis checked him out. Other than the slicked-back dark hair and shiny gray suit, there wasn't much to distinguish the man…except that he appeared to like Cindy, and she liked him.

There wasn't an inch of breathing room between them.

He returned his attention to Rachel, who hadn't stopped watching the pair.

"You think Cindy will get hurt."

"No doubt in my mind."

"There's nothing you can do about it. Cindy's a grown woman and can date anyone she wants."

"I know." She said it grudgingly. It took a moment, but she rallied and showed him her game smile. "I'm okay, Travis. Really."

He led her off the dance floor.

"You need a drink or anything?"

"I'm good. I'm going to head to the ladies' room. Thanks, anyway."

WHEN RACHEL STEPPED out of the washroom, she nearly collided with Nadine.

"I nearly forgot. I have news for you," Nadine said. "I've been doing more digging into Travis."

Rachel's heart sank. "I didn't know you were going to keep looking."

"You know me. I do a job till it's beaten to death. I love doing research."

"You mean you love digging up dirt."

Nadine's broad smile was dazzling. "That, too."

They made room for a couple of women to pass by.

"Seriously, though," Nadine said. "I have news you need to hear." All traces of her good humor had vanished.

"You're scaring me, Nadine. What is it?"

"It's about Travis's sister."

"What about her?"

"Apparently she worked in Las Vegas for some big criminal named Manny D'Onofrio and testified against him. He's in jail now for embezzlement. The scuttlebutt is that he vowed to get revenge."

"Jeepers, Nadine. That sounds like something out of a bad movie."

"I know, but the source was impeccable. Apparently this Manny guy could be quite vicious."

Rachel shivered.

Travis was bringing his sister and her two boys to live in Rodeo, along with whatever danger this *vicious* Manny guy was threatening.

Rachel felt as though she had chips of ice in her veins. Travis had bought the house right across the street from Rachel and her children for his sister. She was coming here to live.

Was she a criminal, too, like her boss? Had she cut a deal to testify against this guy so she wouldn't have to go to jail herself?

Bile rose into Rachel's throat, not morning sickness, but fear.

Travis was bringing danger to her town, to her backyard, to her family.

She knew he wanted them here by Christmas. How close was his sister now?

Was trouble looming on Rachel's doorstep?

Travis was a nice man, a good one, but she would never forgive him for this. None of the kindness he'd shown her in the past could make up for bringing this here.

If she had to fight tooth and nail to protect her family, she would.

If Travis or his sister got in her way, God help them.

"Thanks." Chilled to the bone, she marched away from Nadine to fetch her coat and then to find Travis. "Gotta go."

She located him at the bar set up in the far corner. He nursed a beer.

"Could I talk to you for a minute?"

He raised his eyebrows at her hard-edged tone, but dutifully followed her outside.

In the cool night air, she rounded on him. "What's this I hear about your sister having something to do with a crime in Las Vegas?"

He reared away from her. His expression flattened. "How is that anyone's business but mine?"

"If you bring danger to this town, I have a right to know."

"I'm not bringing *danger*. I'm bringing my sister and her two little kids."

"Your sister worked with a criminal." She'd raised her voice, and a pair of smokers nearby stared at her. "Did she get some kind of deal? What kind of crime was she involved in?"

"She wasn't involved. Only her boss was. She—"

"He said he would come after her."

"He's in jail. Everything will be fine."

She heard defensiveness. Was he protesting too much? She tried to get in his face, but Beth got in the way.

"If any harm comes to my family, I will never forgive you. I will personally boot you and your sister out of my town."

He glowered and hovered over her. She'd never seen him angry and, boy, was he fierce. She stepped back.

He pointed a finger at her. "You know, I thanked you for putting me on that carousel my first day here, but I didn't sign on for a roller-coaster ride. You need to get your emotions together."

"I have every right to defend my family."

He talked over her. "I don't know what's wrong with you, but I don't need this. I'm outta here."

He strode to his truck and drove off. Only once she sat in her own cold vehicle did she realize he'd left without his jacket.

Tough. He could come back for it himself tomorrow.

She no longer cared.

Driven by a need to see Tori, to make sure she was safe and sound, she made it home in record time, following Travis's taillights in the distance.

By the time she turned into her driveway, he was already inside his house.

She paid the babysitter and watched her drive away.

Only after the sitter's car had disappeared down the road did Rachel go to her bedroom doorway to stare at her sleeping daughter.

Tori was safe and sound for now, but how long would that last?

The weight of her duties pressed down on her. Without Davey, she had only herself to rely on to keep her children fed, clothed and sheltered…and to keep them safe.

In this moment, despite all of her constant pep talks to keep her spirits high, she was overwhelmed.

Davey, what have you done to me?

TRAVIS COULDN'T REMEMBER ever being so mad at a woman.

No, that wasn't true. There'd been his last girlfriend, Vivian, who'd turned out to be dishonest and using him.

He'd been furious with her, but this was a different anger altogether.

This was based in fear, in utter terror that Rachel was right—that somehow Manny would find Sammy here. And that Travis truly had brought danger to a town he really liked, and to people he respected.

In his darkened living room, he watched Rachel storm into her trailer. Moments later, the babysitter drove off.

Spooked, he sat watching her home for hours. Nothing moved. No one drove out of the still Montana night to wreak havoc in Rodeo.

In the wee hours of the morning, he forced himself to go to bed.

The following week passed uneventfully. He spent his time alone. On Thanksgiving Day, he stood in his empty home and craved the mayhem of his nephews.

Nothing hollowed out a man like knowing his Thanksgiving dinner would be something pulled out of his freezer. Cardboard turkey, reconstituted mashed potatoes, gluey gravy and cranberry sauce awaited him later this afternoon.

His mood matched the chill wind blowing across the fields. Once the cold had settled on the land in earnest, both color and leaves had been quick to disappear.

There was weather coming in. Travis could feel it.

He stared across the road at the gray metal box hunkered down against the wind. It looked too flimsy to survive much.

Since the dance on the weekend, Cindy's car hadn't reappeared in the driveway. Travis wondered where the new man in town was staying 'cause he was certain that's where Cindy would be found.

How was Rachel doing today?

What kind of Thanksgiving was she having? How was Tori? Was Beth moving a lot?

Travis wouldn't intrude. She'd made her feelings about him clear. She wanted to have nothing more to do with him.

He should want nothing more to do with her.

In his anger he'd been nasty, but he… Well, hell, he might as well admit it. He missed them.

He liked Rachel. He liked her company and her conversation and her smile.

Sick of his own company by eleven in the morning, he made a decision to reach out. He would either be welcome or he'd get a kick in the teeth.

Either way, he'd get a break from himself.

Besides, Ghost needed the company, too.

He shrugged into his sheepskin coat and stepped out into a cold landscape, the unseasonably mild weather of three weeks ago a distant memory.

At Rachel's front door, he screwed up his courage, took a deep breath and knocked.

TRAVIS STOOD ON her doorstep, big and handsome and uncertain of his welcome.

No wonder.

Her emotions were all over the map where this guy was concerned. She could blame it on hormones and the pregnancy, but her basic honesty compelled her to admit the truth.

She liked Travis far more than she should, and it killed her that there was no hope for a future with him.

She was pregnant, he would soon be taking care of his sister and her children, and she didn't want to be anywhere near him if criminal elements came to town.

She'd fumed about it since Nadine had told her about his sister, but today, alone in the trailer with Tori, with nothing but a small turkey breast for their Thanksgiving feast, Rachel was rethinking her stance.

Her mom had been AWOL all week. They might not always get along, but Rachel missed her, especially on this special holiday.

For all intents and purposes, Rachel and Tori were alone. Travis was alone. His sister hadn't arrived yet.

"Would you do me a huge favor?" Travis asked.

He needed a favor? He hadn't yet figured out that she'd give him anything he asked as long as it didn't hurt her or her children?

"What do you need?" she asked.

He ran his fingers through his hair and rested one hand high on the side of the trailer, looking anywhere but at her. His coat gaped open to reveal just a denim shirt underneath. He wore neither hat nor gloves, despite the drop in temperature.

Obviously he'd just run across the road for a brief visit.

"It's a strange request." He picked at a piece of flaking paint with his thumbnail. "Would you and the little one feel like coming over for a couple of hours to help me decorate the house for Christmas?"

Would she?

He was offering her the opportunity to decorate the Victorian for Christmas? He might as well hand her happiness on a silver platter and tie it up with a big red bow.

Would she? Heck, yes!

"Of course." What else could she say? She might have promised herself she would keep her distance from Travis, but turn down the chance to get inside that house and gussy it up? No *way* would she pass that up. "I'd love to help. So would Tori."

"Help what, Mommy?"

Rachel glanced down. Tori had joined her at the door.

"We're going to help Travis decorate his house for Christmas. Would you like that?"

"Yes! We help Travis." She sat on the floor and pulled on her pink cowboy boots. She stood on tiptoe, but couldn't reach her coat. Rachel really needed to hang some low hooks for her.

She handed Tori her winter coat, hat and mittens before donning her own winter gear. The Victorian might be only across the road, but neither Rachel nor Tori was as hardy as Travis seemed to be.

After pulling the front door closed behind her, Rachel followed Travis and Tori across the frozen dirt yard. When crossing the road, Travis held Tori's hand. Rachel approved. She might be trying to keep her emotional distance, but the guy made it hard. He did too much that was right and good.

She stepped into a toasty house. Travis had a fire going. It smelled woodsy, warm and inviting, and so, so much better than the trailer.

Glad to be out of the tin can for a while, she hung her coat and Tori's on the hooks beside the front door.

"You did a beautiful job with the renovations, Travis."

He came to stand beside her in the living room doorway. "Thanks. I tried to keep it true to its roots while modernizing a bit."

The floor was freshly sanded and finished. "I like the color you used on the oak."

"Come in. I want you to see what I did in the kitchen."

She smiled up at him. "If I didn't know better, I'd say you're proud of the house."

A sheepish smile grew on his lips, those beautifully defined lips she'd actually dreamed about.

"Yeah, I guess I kind of am. I've never owned a house before, or a single acre of property."

"You've been caught by the pride-of-ownership bug."

"Maybe. It's for Sammy and my nephews, though. I want them to feel pride. And happiness." He took her elbow to drag her to the kitchen, but she stopped him.

"Wait. I'm savoring all of the changes in here first."

He'd taken all the old layers of paint from the wood trim. Stained dark, it provided a wonderful contrast to the lighter oak of the floors.

She touched a wall. "How did you decide on this sage green for the walls?"

"A woman in the shop helped me."

"Nancy?"

"That was her name."

"She's good with her advice. I like this." She still didn't much like his overstuffed leather couch and armchair in this space, but hey, it was his house. Not hers.

Nonetheless, it was an inviting space. He'd stripped the mantel and wood around the fireplace and had painted it a glossy white. It worked, really brightening the room.

"You did a good job, Travis. I like it."

He towered over her, his heat a source of both balm and sexual irritation, and a real danger to her peace of mind. Good thing he didn't know that.

"That means a lot to me, Rachel. Your opinion matters."

It did? Would wonders never cease? This man kept giving her the sweetest of gifts. Now he offered her his high regard.

Disconcerted by the happiness he brought her, she stepped farther into the room, away from Travis, avoiding trampling her daughter where she sat on the floor, rubbing Ghost's belly.

"Where did this come from? Have you been sewing in the evenings?" She pointed to the rag rug on the hearth, knowing full well he hadn't made it, but it amused her to tease him.

"It came with the house. You wouldn't believe the stuff I've found in different cupboards and nooks and crannies."

"I'll bet Abigail made it. Blue, ivory and rose were her favorite colors."

"That explains all the quilts in those colors."

"She left you quilts?"

"Her family did. At least, they didn't take them when they cleared out the furniture. It seems there was a lot of stuff they didn't want."

"They're distant relatives from England. She didn't have anyone close left. I guess they didn't feel like carting the stuff across the ocean."

"Probably not. In the meantime, I don't own a lot, so I've been using her stuff to fill in the gaps."

Rachel nodded her approval. "You need to update the paintings to your style."

"Trouble is, I don't know what my style is. I know what I don't like, but haven't figured out what I like."

I can help with that. Thank God, she didn't blurt the thought. Travis's life was his. This house was his. Neither had anything to do with her.

And yet…here she was about to help him decorate this house for the holidays. The honor warmed her.

"I'm sure your sister will have ideas of her own. Let's look at your kitchen and then start decorating."

He seemed to like that.

In the kitchen, she pulled up short. Red cupboards dominated white walls.

"Why the red?"

Travis frowned. "Again, Nancy's idea. I told her I wanted color, and she suggested the red. I like it. Don't you?"

He sounded less than confident. Did her opinion matter that much?

"Yes, I do. It surprised me, but you know what? It works."

His frown eased.

To match the cherry-red cabinets, he had placed a few red-and-white-checked items around, a tablecloth and napkins on a large pine table and a couple of dish towels hanging on a rod.

Other than that, very little cluttered the countertops. A toaster designed to look like an old-fashioned radio sat beside a swan-like stainless-steel kettle.

The clean lines served to balance the frivolity of the ornate wood trim, again stained dark here in the kitchen. Surprisingly, it all worked.

She would gladly cook and bake in this kitchen…and that surprised her. She would have gone more traditional to suit the house, but Travis had gone 1950s and had pulled it off.

"I love it."

He exhaled as though he'd been holding his breath.

Tori stepped into the room. "When are we going to decorate?"

"A better question is," Rachel said, "what are we going to use for decorations?"

"I've been looking online for ideas. I never had much of an example when I was a kid." He tucked his hands in his back pockets and, again, Rachel had the sense he was looking for approval. "I thought I could go a little old-fashioned. Plus I don't want to spend a lot of money."

He jerked his chin in the direction of the cabinets. "This renovation stuff is expensive. I need to put a lid on it for now."

"So, what do you have in mind for decorating?"

He opened the plain white refrigerator and pulled out a couple of bags of fresh cranberries. From a cupboard he took a bag of popcorn.

Rachel perked up. "Popcorn and cranberry chains? I love it. So unusual these days."

"Not too old-fashioned?"

She shrugged and held her hands palm up. "Who cares? It's your house, Travis. No one else's. Do what you want."

The side of his mouth quirked up. "Glad it meets with your approval. C'mere."

He left the room, talking over his shoulder. "You liked that Lady Whoever china so much, I think you'll like what I found in the attic."

Small, yellowed boxes sat on the dining-room table, a plain black rectangle with leather parson dining chairs. Again, it wasn't her style, but it wasn't her house, either, was it?

He opened one of the small boxes, and Rachel's breath caught in her throat.

"Ooooh, Travis. You have glass ornaments?"

Jewel-toned balls decorated with hand-painted sparkles nestled in bits of tissue paper.

With his attention on her reaction, Travis said, "It gets even better."

"How can it possibly get any better?"

"Look at these." He lifted the lid from a box, and she was speechless.

Delicate glass birds were nestled into paper muffin cups inside the sectioned box. The intricacy of the painting on the birds left Rachel in awe.

"Travis," she whispered. "Do you realize what you have? These things are worth a fortune."

"I figured since they're so old. I don't want to sell them, though. I want to use them."

Oh, this man. His head was screwed on so right she could hug him. She smiled instead.

"Right answer, Travis. These will be amazing on the tree." She frowned. "You *are* going to have a tree, right? I didn't see one."

"Bought it yesterday. It's thawing in the back porch. Figured you could help put it up."

Again he seemed to be proud of himself, but stumbled when he glanced at her belly.

"On second thought, if you want to start popping corn and stringing it with cranberries, I'll do the heavy lifting with the tree."

She grinned. "I can do that."

She put out her hand, and Tori took it. "Let's go make popcorn, honey."

Travis's kitchen was warm, not drafty like the trailer's, and a pure delight to work in. Every element on the new stove worked.

Tori ate more popcorn than she threaded and broke too many popped kernels when piercing with the blunt needle Rachel had given her. Her lower lip trembled.

"Know what I need you to do, honey?"

"What?"

"What do you see on Travis's walls?"

Tori studied them. "That painting." She pointed to the old-fashioned oil of golden fields.

"What else?"

"Nothing, Mommy."

"Right and that's a real problem. Know why?"

Tori shook her head. "Why?"

"Don't you think it would be nice if Travis had a few pretty drawings to decorate the place?"

"Like in our house?"

"Yes, exactly. Do you feel like coloring a few angels for him?"

"Yeah!" She ran to Travis. "Do you gots paper and crayons?"

"I have computer paper. No crayons, though."

Rachel stood and donned her coat. "I'll get some stuff and be right back."

"It's a bit icy out there. Are you okay crossing the road?"

"I might be eight months pregnant, but I can still walk."

Travis grinned ruefully. "Sorry. I'm working on doing better, Rachel."

With a jaunty wave, she set off for the trailer.

Minutes later, she returned with construction paper, children's scissors, crayons, glue and glitter. Travis was going to hate her for that last item, but what were Christmas decorations without glitter?

After removing her coat, she entered the living room and stared. Like something from a Christmas painting— or from one of her daydreams—Tori sat in the big armchair beside the fire, eating popcorn with Ghost curled on her lap, while Travis, tall and capable, put the finishing touches on the Christmas-tree container. He turned the tree this way and that to find the best aspect.

"What do you think? Is this best?" He turned to her with a smile, and just like that she lost the last of her heart.

She was a goner, completely head over heels in love with a man she couldn't have.

Shaken and stirred, she gripped the back of the sofa and tried to smile.

Chapter Nine

Frowning, Travis took a step toward her. "Are you okay?"

Rachel raised a hand to halt his progress. If he touched her, she might disintegrate into a puddle. She wasn't strong right now. Vulnerable and yearning, she needed to get on more solid footing if she were to survive this day. Or, even more, if she were going to enjoy it.

Travis had given her this gift, and she refused to squander it.

Tamping down on rampant emotions and her most unreasonable desires, she said, "I'm okay, Travis. Just a bit of indigestion. Beth does that to me sometimes."

Didn't that just underscore how unprepared she was for romance…talking about indigestion and pregnancy, of all things. If all of her unrealized daydreams hadn't pierced her heart so badly, she might have laughed at her foolishness.

She smiled, albeit shakily, but rallied and said, "You're right. That is the best aspect of the tree. I like it."

He rubbed his hands. "Okay. Now what? What goes on first?"

"You usually start with threading the lights through the branches, and then we'll add decorations afterward. Do you have lights?"

He picked up a pair of bags from the corner of the living room. The local hardware store's logo graced the sides. "I'll show you what I bought."

Like a magician with a bottomless magic hat, he pulled out boxes of Christmas lights one after another, smaller boxes of white fairy lights, big red pillar candles, a fake greenery wreath and fake snow for the windows.

"Fake snow? Really, Travis?"

She might as well have crushed him. A crestfallen expression crossed his face.

"Oh, hey," she said, rushing to reassure him. "I'm joking! This is going to look awesome in the windows."

He brightened, leaving her to wonder why her opinions were so important to him.

"Here," she said, handing him the lights for the tree. "Start with these."

While he did that, she settled Tori on the floor with the construction paper.

She drew and then cut out a couple of angels, pink and yellow, and handed Tori the crayons to color them.

"Okay," Travis responded. "What do you think of the lights?"

He was on his knees plugging them in, his behind sticking out through the bottom branches. Rachel didn't usually notice men's butts, but Travis had a good one. A great one. Maybe the best male butt on the face of the earth.

Rachel picked up a piece of Tori's construction paper and fanned her face. What was she to do with herself and her inconvenient desire?

The lights on the tree came on, and all thoughts of sex and heat fled.

"Oh, Travis," she said, pressing a hand to her chest. "It's enchanting."

There wasn't a better word for it. Blue lights twinkled in the greenery.

Tori jumped up and ran to him, wrapping her arms around his legs.

"It's pretty, Travis!"

He ruffled her hair. "Glad you like it, sprout."

"Here." Rachel carried over one of the strands of popcorn and cranberries, and they hung it across the front, looping back once.

"Let me get the other strand."

Travis was there ahead of her. When he returned, they looped it across the tree twice below the first strand.

They all stood back.

Blue lights winked behind the red-and-white strands. Even without further decorations the tree was already pretty.

"Let's start adding birds," Rachel said, as excited as a child to see the finished tree.

They were attached to small clips that hooked onto the tree.

"Me, too, Mommy. I want to hang birds." Tori reached for one, but Rachel held back, torn. She didn't like to deny her daughter new experiences, but the birds were fragile, old and valuable.

Travis must have noticed Rachel's hesitation and understood the reason, because he said, "I have a special job for you, Tori. Look."

From one of the hardware store bags he pulled a large gold angel. Tori squealed and clapped her hands.

"Putting this angel on the top of the tree looks like the kind of job you would do just right." Travis asked her to hold it.

She handled it with reverence.

While Rachel clipped birds onto the tree, Travis lifted Tori so she could place the hollow angel right onto the top spire.

They stood back and admired it.

Rachel had finished the birds and had started on the equally delicate glass balls.

To preempt Tori from touching them, Travis asked, "Hey, weren't you making angels for me? Where are they?"

"Here!" She gathered her angels and handed them to him.

"Well, now, these are beautiful, but you've left me in a real quandary."

"What's a quand?"

"In a real jam. I don't know where to hang them. Help me out here and show me the best spots."

Tori rose to the occasion and had Travis hang them around the room. The fact that every spot was only three or four feet off the floor, in other words, at Tori's level, didn't seem to bother Travis one bit.

The way he valued Tori and considered her opinions was another of the things that Rachel lov—liked about him.

Oh, who was she kidding? She loved him.

There was no denying her heart's desire, but boy, did it hurt that life hadn't turned out differently.

Why her life had ended up the way it had was a mystery to her. All she could do was hold on tightly to her belief that she would survive, and she would raise her daughters to be the best people they could possibly be.

One way or another, she would give them a good chance. She hadn't figured out how yet, but their lives would be better than hers.

There would be no fighting in their home. It might be only a tin can, temporarily, but with Cindy shacked up with the new man in town at the moment, there was peace.

By late afternoon, they'd finished decorating.

"I guess it's time for us to go home." Rachel didn't want this glorious day to end. Not yet. Soon enough she could return to the reality of her life alone.

Travis glanced out of the window toward her trailer,

sitting in the falling darkness. Dusk came so early at this time of year.

"We could, you know, maybe have supper together," he said.

Was it possible that he didn't want things to end so soon, either?

"I could pick us up a pizza." Travis interrupted her thoughts. "What would you think of that?"

"Pizza! Yeah!" Tori clapped her hands.

How much did she have in her wallet? Could she offer to help pay? Payday wasn't until next week.

As though reading her mind, he said, "It's my treat. You helped me decorate." He glanced around his living room. If she weren't mistaken, Rachel would almost think he looked emotional. "The least I can do is spring for pizza."

He pulled up short. "Darn. It's Thanksgiving. Everything will be closed."

"The pizza shop next to the new mall is open every day."

"Good." Travis rubbed his hands together.

"How about if Tori and I go home and get her bathed for the night while you drive into town? That way she'll be ready for bed when I get her back home later."

"Perfect. I'll leave the front door open. C'mon back when you're ready."

They discussed toppings and Travis drove off.

Rachel and Tori went home and did their thing. With Tori clean and dressed in warm flannel pjs, they put on their coats and headed back to Travis's house.

Kneeling by the fireplace in the living room, Rachel stirred the ashes to life and built the blaze back up again.

They'd done a great job of decorating the mantel with fake greenery threaded with fairy lights and red pillar candles. A good day's work. Satisfaction and happiness flooded her.

Travis had given her a real gift today.

Whistling, she carried the milk and hot chocolate she'd brought over to the kitchen to make hot chocolate for Tori.

Ensconced in front of the fire and covered with a colorful afghan from the back of the sofa, Tori curled up with Ghost.

Just as Rachel put the half-full mug of warm chocolate into Tori's hands, the doorbell rang.

"Who on earth?" Maybe Travis had his hands full and couldn't turn the doorknob.

Rachel opened the door and stared. A beautiful woman stood on the veranda.

Tall and slim, in a long, white, wool coat, she might be the most sophisticated visitor to ever come to town.

A white scarf shot with gold thread cradled a firm jawline and a white-fur hat framed a heart-shaped face.

The only color, her bright red lips, popped against all of that stunning white.

She looked like a model from a magazine.

Rachel combed her fingers through her hair, aware that she came up short in comparison to this goddess.

"Oh!" the woman said. "I thought this was the address for Travis Read."

"It is. This is his house."

A tiny frown formed between dark brows. "You live here?"

Rachel shook her head. "We're visiting."

"Is Travis home?"

"Not at the moment. He'll be back soon." Should she invite her in? Rachel liked to be polite, but this wasn't her home.

"I'm a friend of his," the woman said.

When Rachel vacillated, the woman continued, "A *very* good friend. I'm anxious to see him again. It's been a couple of months."

Rachel understood immediately, but Travis hadn't mentioned a girlfriend.

A light bulb went off. Her thoughts traveled back to the day Travis had kissed her so sweetly and thoroughly after crashing his bike.

This paragon of womanly sophistication must have been who Travis was really kissing, not Rachel with her late husband's clothes and big belly.

She stepped aside and the woman entered.

"I'm Rachel McGuire. I live across the road."

"Vivian Hughes." She took off her coat and hung it on one of the hooks. Next, off came the hat. Long, straight, jet-black hair hung down her back.

Beside her Rachel felt gauche. Funny, until Travis had come to town, she'd never worried about her appearance. These days, it seemed that was all she did.

The realization bothered her.

Pull yourself together, Rachel. You aren't that shallow.

No, she wasn't, but sometimes her pride smarted.

"This is my daughter, Victoria."

Tori stared wide-eyed and lifted her hand in a tiny wave.

On closer inspection in the living-room lighting, the woman wasn't so perfect, after all.

She was older than Rachel had thought at first, closer to Cindy's age than to her own. Tiny wrinkles radiated from the outer corners of her eyes. The black of her hair was just a shade too dark for the woman's eyebrows. So not real.

Vivian sat on the sofa and checked out the room, her eyes resting on Tori's crude but colorful angels hung around the room.

"Cozy," she murmured, and Rachel wasn't sure whether she referred to the room or to a perceived relationship between her and Travis.

Travis entered the house.

"Hey, who owns that sleek little BMW in the driveway?"

"Travis," Tori called. "You got comp'ny. We been taking care of her."

Rachel heard him toe off his boots. She held her breath. Just who was this Vivian to him? Just how *very* close were they?

Travis entered the room and, to Rachel's satisfaction, did not look happy to see Vivian.

So small, Rachel. So mean-spirited.

So honest.

"Viv," he said, voice flat. "What are you doing here?"

Vivian stood and, for the first time since arriving, did not look cool and collected.

"We need to talk, Travis."

His lips thinned. "We already said everything that needed to be said. There's nothing else."

Okay, this was uncomfortable. Rachel did not want to be here for this kind of conversation.

"Tori and I should go," she said.

"No. I got pizza. You're not going home without dinner."

"This kind of conversation should be just between the two of you, Travis."

"There isn't going to be any of *that* kind of conversation, is there, Viv?"

"You're right, Travis," Vivian answered. "This isn't about us."

"Why are you here, then?"

Vivian twisted her fingers, the red of her nails an exact match to her lipstick. She bit her bottom lip for a second. "It's about Manny."

Everything inside Rachel froze. *Manny.* The criminal Travis's sister had worked for was Manny D'Onofrio, Nadine had said. He was *vicious.* He vowed revenge.

"What about him?" Her hard-edged voice could cut through steel.

Both Vivian and Travis stared at her.

"He's the criminal from Las Vegas, right?"

Vivian nodded.

"What attachment do you have to him? Who *are* you?"

"I'm Travis's girlfriend."

Travis stepped forward. "Not for well over a year, Vivian."

"But I hoped—"

"No, Viv. There is no hope. I made that clear months ago in Vegas."

"I thought you seemed open to starting over."

"Telling you I was ready to forgive you for your betrayal is not the same as saying I want to start over."

Rachel didn't care about any of that. She had only one concern.

"Is Manny coming here?" Her granite tone rattled them. Rachel sensed Tori's bewilderment as she watched the adults.

"He's in jail," Vivian said.

Rachel looked at Travis.

"He has men, employees who are loyal to him," he admitted.

He turned his attention to Vivian. "Are they coming here?"

She nodded.

Blood frigid, Rachel scrambled to get her daughter out of this house before a band of criminals with guns landed on the doorstep.

"Mommy, I want more hot chocolate," Tori complained.

Fingers numb, she buttoned Tori into her jacket. "You'll have some more at home."

"But the pizza…" Travis's expression pleaded with her to…what? Stay? Ignore the danger?

"But what if someone shows up to…" She trailed off. She didn't want to scare Tori.

"It isn't going to happen this second, Rachel."

"How do you know?"

He opened his mouth. Closed it. How could he know when these guys planned to arrive?

"I can't stay here, Travis." Frantic to get away, she shoved her arms into her coat and opened the door. Crossing the road, she made herself slow down for Tori's sake.

Once inside her own home, she locked the door and shoved a kitchen chair under the knob. Her teeth chattered.

"Mommy?" Tori's lower lip trembled. "What's wrong?"

Rachel forced herself to get control. The very last thing she wanted was to scare her daughter. All she asked for was that her children be safe and have enough to eat.

She made herself smile. "Let's watch TV, okay?"

Tori immediately said, "'Kay," and ran to her favorite chair, a child-size blue plush armchair, one of Cindy's purchases. Some of Rachel's fear must have transferred, though, because Tori picked up her platypus and held her extra tightly.

Rachel flipped through the channels until she found a sappy Thanksgiving movie suitable for family entertainment.

Aware of Vivian across the road bringing bad news, Rachel jumped at every sound the gusting wind made. Again, she felt the full weight of her responsibility.

For the first time since Davey's death, she let go of her grief and gave in fully to her anger. She'd loved Davey, but he should have been careful. He should have thought of his family.

He should have loved her and Tori more than he loved his fun.

ALL OF THE joy drained out of Travis's hitherto amazing day, leached out by this lousy excuse for a woman. What the heck was Vivian doing here?

Where Rachel was comfortable in an oversize men's gray sweatshirt, round in pregnancy and as honest as the day was long, Vivian was thin and fashionable…and the most dishonest, betraying woman on the face of the earth.

The sound of the front door closing behind Rachel and Tori angered him even as he was filled with remorse.

He should have never come here and brought his troubles with him, so close to her and her kids.

Oh, jeez. Damn it all to crap. His heart ached like he'd lost something precious and rare.

Travis turned to the woman he didn't trust and might possibly hate more than Manny D'Onofrio—at least Manny had never hidden who he was. "Stay put," he ordered. "I'll be right back."

He deposited the smaller of the two pizzas in the kitchen and carried the larger one across the road.

He knocked, but no one answered. Figuring Rachel might have been spooked, he called, "Rachel, it's me. I brought pizza."

He heard noise on the other side of the door, and then it opened.

Rachel stood beside a chair she had obviously slid in front of the door to protect them. The hollow, fearful look in her eyes worried him.

"You didn't have to bring that over."

He shoved it into her hands, not giving her a chance to resist. "Yes, I did. You and Tori worked hard. I promised you dinner. Here it is."

"Okay."

"Rachel, I'm not going to let anything happen to you."

Her backbone kicked in. "I can take care of Tori and me. You just worry about yourself and your girlfriend."

"She's not my girlfriend."

Rachel held up her hand. "Please, Travis, just go. I'm too tired for this."

He could see she was. "Okay, but call me if you need me."

"Yeah." She closed the door firmly, and he knew she wouldn't call him for any reason.

He stomped back across the road to confront Vivian Hughes.

He'd thought he'd loved her once, but there was a huge leap between lust and love. He'd certainly trusted her, but that was before he'd found out she was working for Manny, keeping an eye on him, hoping to find out anything about Samantha that Manny could supply to his defense team.

How on earth any of that intelligence could have helped Manny's embezzlement case, Travis didn't understand. Trying to find dirt on Samantha to discredit her as a witness, perhaps? Maybe he just wasn't devious enough to figure it out.

To say he was mad put it mildly. Furious was more like it. And terrified.

"How did you find me?" he demanded.

Vivian's gaze slid away from his. "Remember when we said goodbye last year? How angry you were?"

He nodded.

"You made me so mad. When I asked to see you three months ago to apologize for betraying you to Manny, it was really to betray you again."

He couldn't speak, not for the life of him, or he would spew all kinds of filth.

"I was only pretending to be sorry," she said. She looked sorry now, but he didn't care. "I really went there to stick a tracker onto your truck. I've been monitoring your travels. When you remained here for a while, I figured maybe this was where you planned to settle and bring Samantha."

"What? *Why?*"

"Manny asked me to." She shrugged, and the gesture was delicate and feminine, but at the moment, he could gladly throttle her. He shoved his hands into his pockets. "I told him where you are."

"Did his men come with you?"

"No. I left right after I told Manny. He said good job, paid me and told me to leave."

He had to warn Sammy not to come. Where could he send her? Fury flooded him, chasing out the ice with a white-hot flame. All of his work in finding this town, this house, had gone up in smoke because of Vivian.

Travis couldn't get his phone out of his pocket fast enough. He fumbled, dropping it onto the carpet.

"Travis, I—" She approached, but he held up a hand.

"Keep away from me, or so help me God I won't be responsible for my actions." He dialed Sammy's number. "Betraying me the first time was bad enough when it only hurt me. This time you'll be hurting my sister and her boys."

Sammy's phone rang, but she didn't answer. Travis cursed. "You're lucky I'm not a violent man."

Travis cut the connection. He dialed Cole Payette's number.

"Hey, Travis." Cole answered on the second ring. "What's up?"

"I got a person here at the house who needs to be escorted out of town."

"But—" Vivian interrupted.

Travis shushed her.

"Does this relate to the situation with your sister?"

"It sure does. I'll call her and tell her not to come to Rodeo. In the meantime, the woman in my house is a danger to me, to my family and to everyone else in town."

"No, I'm not." Vivian no longer sounded scared, but she was starting to heat up. Too bad. He didn't care about her feelings.

"I'll be right there." Cole disconnected. Great sheriff. Great town.

He thought of Rachel across the road, angry with him

for bringing danger to her home. She was good people. The best. And he was so damned sorry he couldn't be the type of man she needed. Instead, he was the kind who attracted people like Vivian and Manny.

He phoned Samantha again. Still no response. Where was she?

She wasn't due to leave San Francisco yet. Maybe her battery was dead. Sammy could be impulsive. It would be like her to come early to surprise him.

He prayed to God she wouldn't cross paths with Manny's men.

Cursing, he turned his attention to Vivian.

"Why?" he asked.

"Why what?"

"Why did you betray me to Manny not once, but twice?" He'd thought he'd buried the hurt, but seeing her again brought it flooding back.

"For money, Travis. Manny gave me a lot of money. Tons. I'll be secure for years to come."

Money. Worse than the anger was the grief.

She'd killed a love he'd thought was special, strong enough to inspire the most momentous decision he'd ever made.

He'd never contemplated marriage before Vivian. He had never believed it was for him. But for a brief time, he'd thought the two of them could make it work.

Hold on. Be honest. You were leading up to asking her, but you never did, did you? Why did you hold back? Was it really love?

Had he known on some level that there were problems, with Vivian or himself or the relationship?

Travis called Sammy again. No answer. He tossed the phone onto the sofa.

Brooding, he stared at Vivian.

She watched him silently. What did she want from him?

He thought of a question he should have asked at the start. "Why are you here?"

"To warn you." She spread her hands as though to say, Isn't it obvious?

It wasn't. Where Viv was concerned, nothing was as it seemed.

"Why? You betrayed me to Manny, twice now, and all of a sudden you're on my side warning me?" He startled and headed for the door. "Are they here? Are they waiting outside for me to lead them to Sammy?"

She rushed after him and grabbed his arm. "No, they aren't anywhere near here yet. I was telling the truth."

He stared at the well-manicured hand on his sleeve. "I don't understand."

"All along I felt bad about the way I was using you."

"You slept with me. Did your job description include whoring for your boss?"

She shrank from him. "No. I liked you. I was attracted to you. I wanted to sleep with you. Manny gave me hell for it after you left, along with a black eye. He was jealous."

"Is that supposed to make me feel sorry for you?"

"No. Just understand. I truly cared for you, Travis. You're a good, good man." Her voice deepened with intensity. "You're a better man than Manny will ever be. After I told him where you were now, I was so ashamed. Your sister did the right thing when she testified against him. You're innocent. Your sister had no idea what she was getting into when she went to work for him. Neither of you deserve Manny's revenge."

Was she telling the truth? Hard to say. She'd seemed sincere in the past, too.

The sound of tires on gravel alerted Travis. He peeked through the window and breathed a sigh when he saw it was the sheriff.

Had it been Manny's people, he would have fought to

the death rather than tell where Sammy was, but then who would be left to protect her and the boys?

A split second before Cole knocked on the door, Travis opened it.

"Thanks for coming."

Cole nodded. "No worries. This her?" He gestured toward Vivian.

"Yeah. Vivian Hughes. She works for Manny D'Onofrio."

Cole turned a cold eye on her. "I did some research after our talk. He's a nasty piece of work. You work for him?"

Vivian lifted her chin. "Not anymore. I quit. I came to warn Travis about his men coming here."

"I have no way to verify whether you're telling the truth. Travis says you're a danger to the town and its people. I believe him. I'm going to ask you to leave."

Vivian turned her gaze to Travis. Her eyes shimmered like jewels behind her tears.

He wasn't moved. The thing about trust was that once broken, it couldn't be repaired.

"That's it?" she asked.

"What were you expecting?"

She shrugged, but this time he wasn't fooled. She wasn't indifferent. She wanted him back. She'd actually thought this would be enough to fix things between them.

She'd thought she could take Manny's money *and* have Travis.

There wasn't enough glue in the entire state of Montana to fix what Vivian had broken. She just didn't understand that.

"It's over, Vivian. There's nothing between us. Are you telling the truth about the people coming to town?"

"Yes."

"Then, I thank you for that. You did the right thing. But I hope to God I never see you again."

"Fine." She swallowed hard. At the front door, she looked back once before heading to her car.

Cole said, "I'll see that she leaves. I'll follow her for a while to make sure she doesn't double back."

Travis shook his hand. "I appreciate this, Cole. We don't need her kind in Rodeo."

The sheriff turned up his collar against the rising wind. "Batten down the hatches, Read. There's a major storm moving in."

"Will do." Travis agreed, recognizing that the menacing sky on the horizon was a harbinger of more than just bad weather. It also represented the havoc Manny had let loose in sending his men to Rodeo, Montana.

Chapter Ten

With the weather forecast on her mind, Rachel bundled up Tori and took her into town to buy groceries.

There was a storm coming in, due any minute. Rachel wanted the fridge and pantry as full as she could afford.

She owned a small wind-up radio in the event of a power outage so she could keep on top of news and weather reports. In her bedside table, she kept a flashlight.

When she got home, she'd pile the bed with her blankets and all of Cindy's, in case of a power failure. She and Tori could snuggle together, and Cindy wasn't home to use them anyway.

Rachel still hadn't seen her mother since the dance. She'd called and had left a message, but Cindy hadn't returned her call.

It hurt that her mom wouldn't even check in to see how they were doing. Sure, Rachel had always been independent, and possessed more common sense than the thimbleful rolling around in Cindy's brain, but why couldn't Cindy exhibit the least bit of motherly concern?

Rachel bought mostly dry goods. If they lost power, she wouldn't be able to cook anyway. She stocked up on bread and rolls, peanut butter and jam, and cartons of shelf-stable almond milk. Dry cereal would do for now.

They drove home with Tori warbling away with the songs on the radio. Rachel never tired of her sweet high voice.

In the unrelenting dull gray of the day, the trailer looked abandoned when Rachel drove up.

She carried the groceries inside with Tori trailing behind.

She didn't bother jamming a chair under the front door-knob. What were the chances of anyone coming to her crummy little trailer after finding Travis in his own house?

Last night's panic had given way to common sense.

She set the bags on the kitchen counter.

Rachel got Tori set up in front of the small TV and put away the groceries.

After every last item was in its proper place, she headed to her bedroom to put away the three pairs of thick socks she'd gotten on sale for Tori.

In a space as small as the trailer, everything had to be put away the second after you were finished using it.

But when she opened the door, she stopped dead. At the sight of her bedroom turned upside down, with everything topsy-turvy, her jaw dropped. It had been trashed.

Oh my God, they'd been robbed.

She started back to the kitchen to call the sheriff, but halted in Cindy's doorway, caught by the sight of empty drawers.

Not trashed or turned over drawers, but *empty* drawers.

She stepped inside.

This was no robbery. This was Cindy leaving. Rachel checked the closet. Cindy's one suitcase was missing.

Her mom had—

Rachel's legs gave out, and she sat heavily on the bed.

Her mom had left.

There was no other explanation. She had packed her bag and had headed out of town without a single word to her family.

In the bathroom, all of Cindy's toiletries were gone, including the expensive creams she'd taken to using lately.

Why had she ransacked Rachel's room? Cindy owned a lot more clothes than Rachel did, and they were a lot prettier.

Back in her own room, the truth hit her like a wrecking ball, sending shards of Rachel's life flying.

Rachel had been robbed after all, by her own mother.

The items from the top shelf of her closet, behind which Rachel had hidden her boxes of Mason jars full of the change she'd scrimped and saved over the years, were strewed on the floor.

Her money, five thousand dollars' worth of sacrifices, was gone.

Dizzy, she stumbled before realizing she'd been holding her breath. She lay down on the bed. Stars danced behind her closed eyelids.

Before she could stop them, tears leaked from her eyes, little bits of ice shaking free of the iceberg her heart had become.

Rachel would have expected betrayal from a lot of people, but never her own mother. Not Cindy.

What on earth was she going to do?

She should have rolled every last coin and counted every single small bill and deposited it all in the bank. She'd gotten into the habit of hiding the money from Davey and had never changed that after his death.

She'd been a fool.

After Davey's death, it hadn't taken her long to realize she would need to use some of her down-payment money to support herself and her children after Beth was born.

Now Cindy was gone and had taken her money.

How would she buy food? How would she pay the hospital after she gave birth to Beth? Her limited health insurance wouldn't cover everything, and her credit rating was still recovering from Davey's extravagant spending habits. Would the hospital even accept her credit card?

Her head stopped spinning, but her breathing was still

shallow. She made herself breathe deeply, evenly. She couldn't manage normal, though. Not when her life had just been shattered.

It would never be normal again.

At least there was no mortgage on the trailer.

Her heart clenched.

Or was there?

Would Cindy have borrowed against the trailer before leaving? Surely the bank wouldn't be that foolish. But she'd had a week since meeting that man to plan all kinds of weird and foolish things.

Was she even with him anymore? After all, that was only an assumption on Rachel's part and the product of gossip in town.

A swift kick to her ribs alerted her to Beth's discomfort. She stood carefully and paced, sidestepping the clothes and mess on the floor.

Thinking over Cindy's actions at the dance, running away with the stranger was the only explanation.

A spot of bright pink on her bedside table caught her eye. A note.

It's time for me to live for myself. You're strong. I'm not. I need a man. Gerry's good to me. You know how to live on less money. You'll be okay.

Oh, Mom. Yet again, she was making a fool of herself over a man. The more things changed, the more they stayed the same.

Rachel swiped tears from her cheeks fiercely. She had to stop crying for Tori's sake. Tears accomplished *nothing*.

Angry with herself and her mother and life, Rachel's pacing changed to stomping.

With no other outlet, without the option to scream until her grief and rage ran dry, she stomped.

Oh, how she stomped.

If the floor of the trailer caved in, tough.

She stomped out to the front doorway, where she'd set a baseball bat in case she needed it. She clutched it and tramped back to her bedroom, closing the door so Tori wouldn't hear.

This crappy trailer, this hollow life, Cindy's dishonesty, Davey's carelessness, came crashing in on her.

With the bat as her weapon, she pounded her mattress, keening low in her throat. She hit it again…and again… and again, over and over until her arms ached.

She'd been good. She'd been kind and thoughtful and giving. She'd been the best person she could possibly be, yet these people and this life had dumped all over her. And she was furious.

She pounded the mattress until her rage died, until she fell limply against the side of the bed.

Since his death, she had grieved Davey, had cried buckets with the pain of missing him, but hadn't fully acknowledged her anger. What kind of woman would be angry with a man who had died far too young? Her. She'd been enraged, but had buried it.

"You should have cared more about me and Tori," she whispered, swiping tears from her cheeks. "Now, we're alone."

If tears were bad, self-pity was worse.

Buck up. You have a beautiful daughter here and another on the way. Count your damned blessings.

What she wanted more was to count the money she'd put away for the next few months. What was she supposed to do now?

Drained, but strangely cleansed, she rested the baseball bat in the corner and trudged to the kitchen to make a couple of grilled cheese sandwiches.

RACHEL TRIED TO pull herself together for Tori's sake.

Even though she didn't know how they would survive,

Rachel understood she had to do her best for her child. She stroked her belly. Correction, her children.

Outside, the wind howled and snow beat against the windows. The storm had hit fast and hard.

After cleaning up the mess Cindy had made of her bedroom, Rachel put Tori to bed.

Giving Tori an amazing Christmas became her top priority, but how? How could she buy presents?

She stiffened her resolve. There was always a way. She couldn't purchase gifts, but she could make them.

Scouring the trailer for ideas, she found a stash of yarn left over from one of Cindy's failed attempts at domesticity.

Rachel sat on the sofa and cast on to knit a pair of bright pink mittens for Tori. Cindy might not have had a talent for crafts, but her mother had. Rachel had learned many things from her grandma. Knitting was one of them.

The first mitten went quickly because Tori's hands were so tiny. A couple of hours later, Rachel had finished it and was casting on to start the second one when a bad case of indigestion hit.

Funny. All they'd had for dinner was grilled cheese sandwiches and tinned tomato soup, a simple meal she'd eaten hundreds of times before without problems.

She rubbed her tummy. "Beth, honey, you're messing with Mommy's body."

Her discomfort slowed her down.

A while later, it got worse. When her first contraction hit, she panicked.

The problem wasn't her tummy. It was Beth. The baby wanted to come.

No.

Not now. No. The timing couldn't possibly be worse. She was a week early. The storm was vast, moving down from the north across the entire state.

Another pain and she dropped her knitting.

In her bedroom, she woke Tori. Scrambling with fumbling hands, she dragged her own small suitcase out of the closet, packed and ready for the trip to the hospital.

Another contraction tightened her belly, and she gasped.

"Hurry." She nudged Tori. "Wake up, honey, please. Beth is coming."

Tori sat up and rubbed her eyes. "From where, Mommy?"

"From my tummy. Remember I told you about it? It's going to happen now."

"I'm sleepy. Tell Beth to wait until morning."

Despite her nerves, Rachel laughed. "I wish she would wait, too."

Nervously, she glanced out the window. The wind lashed a solid film of snow against the glass. By morning, the storm might have abated, but the roads wouldn't be any clearer. It would take days to clean up this mess.

Still, she had to brave the drive. She had no choice.

What to do with Tori now that Cindy was gone? Surely, she could depend on one of her friends. Maybe Honey? Yes. Honey would take her in a heartbeat.

Okay. First, Rachel would drive into town to drop her daughter off with Honey above the tavern.

Next she would drive to the hospital, but that was a twenty-minute drive on a good day. Tonight it would take—

Snow beat against the thin walls of the trailer. It could take hours, if she made it there at all.

She wasn't too proud to admit she was scared. Terrified.

She tried to phone Honey, but there was no signal.

Another contraction hit. She bent over and held her breath until it passed.

"Please hurry, Tori. We need to go."

"Go where?"

"I'm taking you to stay with Honey before I go to the hospital."

Reacting to the tension Rachel couldn't hide, Tori climbed out of bed and dressed.

Rachel threw her clothes into her little knapsack. "Do you want Puss?"

"Yes, Mommy, please. Puss likes Honey."

Translation…Tori liked Honey. Rachel breathed a sigh of relief. Everything would be fine.

Her optimism lasted through getting them both into their winter clothes and stepping out through the front door, where the wind knocked them back into the trailer.

Dear Lord, it was a bad one.

With Tori's knapsack on her back and her own suitcase in her left hand, she grasped Tori's hand firmly and pushed them both against the wind.

"Hold on to my pant leg while I close the door." The wind whipped the words out of her mouth. "Tori? Tori, can you hear me?"

Rachel bent over and wrapped Tori's tiny fingers around her pant leg. Against the side of her hat, she yelled, "Hold on tightly. Don't let go. Okay?"

Tori nodded.

"Look at me, Tori."

Her daughter looked up, but closed her eyes against the snow buffeted by the relentless wind. "Don't let go at all. Do you understand?"

"Yes, Mommy." The wind carried off her voice, thin and sounding scared to be outside in a raging snowstorm, but Rachel was assured Tori understood.

Only then did she pull the door closed and retrieve Tori's hand and hold it tightly.

Not only the wind, but also contractions robbed Rachel of breath. She figured they were only three minutes apart already—so much faster than with Tori.

How could this be happening?

She could only barely make out the car through the swirling snow.

The drive would be bad, slow and treacherous. Even if she managed to stay on the road, it would take her two, three times longer to get to town, never mind to the hospital miles away.

Did she have that long?

Another contraction hit, answering with a resounding no.

She looked around wildly. She couldn't possibly give birth alone in the trailer. No way was her daughter starting her life in that tin can—but if not there, where? Rachel really had no choice. But what would she do with Tori? She didn't want her daughter more frightened than she already was.

A light flickered across the road, hardly visible.

Travis was home.

Tori would be safe with him in the Victorian while Rachel gave birth in the trailer.

Rachel's independence had carried her far, but it was time to ask for help for her daughter's sake. She couldn't think of a single person she would rather run to for help at this moment than solid, dependable Travis Read.

"Change of plans, Tori," she shouted. "You're going to stay with Travis."

"'Kay." Tori huddled against Rachel's leg. "I like Travis. So does Puss."

"Let's go."

By hook or by crook, Rachel was getting Tori safely across the road to Travis and into the Victorian where she had always found safety and solace.

They trudged across the road. It took forever. Rachel's focus never swayed from that one yellow light in the living room window. She knew, even if her daughter couldn't understand, that they were perilously close to getting lost out here in the storm. Without that light to guide them, they could easily veer off course and freeze to death just feet from shelter.

The snow was thickening and the wind becoming worse. She didn't relish the trip back to the trailer alone.

At last, they reached the porch. Rachel knocked, the wood hurting her frozen knuckles through her gloves.

The door opened and there he was, the man she knew would protect Tori with his life. Relief flooded her.

She'd been wrong to say all of those nasty things to him. Travis would never knowingly hurt another human being. He never would have come here if he'd thought trouble would follow him.

His dear face registered surprise followed by alarm when she gasped and grasped her belly.

"Rachel, what the hell?"

"Travis, I'm cold," Tori said.

"Get in here."

He lifted Tori into his arms, then grabbed Rachel's hand and dragged her inside. When the suitcase banged against the doorjamb and she dropped it, he ordered, "Leave it. I'll get it."

Once he had them safely indoors, he went back for the suitcase and slammed the door against the wind that was forcing snow inside, even with the deep porch attempting to offer protection.

He carried Tori into the living room where a glorious fire burned in the grate.

Undressing her with care, he said, "What on earth are you doing out in this weather? Only a fool would leave home in this."

"Then I'm a fool." Rachel was so far past tired she didn't have the energy to quarrel with him. The stress of her mother's betrayal weighed on her like a ton of bricks, and she still had to get back across the street to give birth.

"You got that right." Travis sounded angry, but he handled Tori with a gentle touch. He set her up in an armchair and hauled it right in front of the fire.

Ghost ambled over and jumped up beside her.

"Kitty!" Tori said around a huge yawn.

His startled gaze took in Tori's pajamas.

To Rachel, he said, "You got her out of bed. Why?"

Rachel couldn't answer, but leaned on the back of the sofa and breathed hard through a contraction.

In an instant, Travis was by her side rubbing her back. "What's wrong?"

His hand felt so good, she ordered, "Harder."

"What?"

"Press harder. Right there. Yes, that's good. Press harder! Yesssss."

"Rachel." She caught a warning note in his voice. "What's going on?"

"Can you take care of Tori for a little while?"

"Of course, but why? Where are you going?"

"Back home for a while."

"Back home? Whoa. Wait." He watched her double over. "Are you—? Is the baby—? Sweet Jesus, you're in labor, aren't you?"

Rachel panted. "A bit early. Can't drive to hospital in this. Don't want Tori to hear if…it gets bad."

"It already looks bad."

She shot him a small smile. "This is nothing, Travis."

"Does Cindy know how to deliver a baby?"

Rachel shied away from the truth. Travis didn't need to know that Cindy had left. "She's had a baby. I've had one. Everything will work out."

Oh, she didn't want to be alone—she really didn't—but neither did she want Travis pitying her, or feeling responsible for her. He might be superdependable, but the guy had his hands full with a sister and two nephews coming to town.

Rachel meant nothing to him.

"Put Tori to bed if you have a spare one. Or the sofa is fine."

She opened Tori's knapsack and handed Puss to Travis. She picked up her suitcase and headed for the door.

"I'll be back in the morning."

Fingers crossed. She hoped it would be a fast labor. It sure felt like it would be.

With a deep, fortifying breath she stepped outside and pulled the door closed behind her. She climbed down from the veranda to start the loneliest walk of her life.

Chapter Eleven

Travis stared at the closed door.

What the hell had just happened?

He turned to Tori who was falling asleep near the fire and picked her up.

"We'd better get you into a bed."

"'Kay."

"Is your mom really having her baby tonight?"

"Uh-huh." The child nodded against his shoulder. "She said Beth is coming."

"Cindy knows what to do, right?" he asked, though why he expected a sleepy three-year-old to be able to answer that was beyond him.

"Cindy's not home, Travis. Mommy said she ranned away."

"She *what?*"

"Cindy ranned away. Mommy will be alone. Why did she putted me here and go back alone?"

Travis cursed internally. "Good question."

He would give Rachel an earful about this later, but for now he had to drag her back here with him.

He plopped Tori into the armchair, said, "Wait here," and shrugged into his sheepskin jacket.

When he threw open the door, the wind smacked him in the face. Why did this hyper-independent, ornery woman think it was all right to give birth alone in an empty trailer when she had a perfectly good friend right across the street who would do anything to help her out?

Including helping her to give birth? His gut clenched.

Yeah, including that.

He'd think about the details once he had Rachel safe with him.

He jumped down from the veranda and nearly ran into her.

A sob escaped her. "I can't do it, Travis. I can't give birth alone. Help me. Please."

Thank God! He yanked her against his chest. She was safe! She'd changed her mind.

Inside his house, he slammed the door behind her and threw his shearling jacket onto a hook. He turned to give her a piece of his mind, but halted. She looked miserable.

"I'm sorry."

"Why? For needing my help?"

She reacted to his harshness by shaking her head. "No, for all of the nasty things I've said and thought about you lately."

"Aw, hell. Don't worry about it. I understand."

He took her coat from her and hung it up. Gently, he took her arm to lead her into the living room when Rachel gasped.

A great spurt of liquid gushed from her. Travis jumped out of the way. "What the he—"

"My water's broken. It won't be long now."

His hands started to shake. "What do you need me to do?"

"Get Tori into bed first, preferably behind a closed door."

"You got it."

"C'mon, munchkin." Tori didn't hear him. "She's already out like a light."

"She's a heavy sleeper."

He gathered her, Puss and Ghost into his arms and carried them upstairs to the bedroom he'd set up for the boys, gently placing her in one of the twin beds and covering her with ample blankets. He tucked Puss under her arm.

Ghost circled and lay beside her.

Travis closed the door.

Back downstairs he ran to the kitchen and put on a huge pot of water to boil.

"What are you doing?" Rachel asked.

"I don't know. That's what they do in the movies."

Her skin was pale and her cheeks flushed, but she smiled. "Get me some old rags and I'll clean up my mess in the hallway."

Outrage filled him. "Stop that kind of talk. I'll take care of it, but first, we need to get you settled in. Where? In my bed?"

"No, birthing's a messy business. I don't want to ruin your new mattress."

"I don't care," he said harshly.

She touched his arm. "I do. Do you have any extra blankets?"

"The linen closet is full of old quilts. I haven't touched them. They're probably dusty."

"Those will be Abigail's homemade quilts. She will have taken good care of them over the years. Let me see them."

She chose three large thick ones and a whole bunch of old towels.

Without warning, she leaned against him and breathed heavily. Panted. Moaned. "God," she said.

"Contraction?" he asked.

She rode it out and nodded. "Bring all of that to the living room. We need to get me settled in. Quickly."

He followed her, asking, "How can you be so calm?"

"Because I've done it before. If this were my first, it would be different."

He started to spread the quilts on the sofa, but she shook her head.

"No, here."

"On the floor? Are you out of your mind?"

"The floor can be cleaned up easily."

"I'm not letting you give birth on the floor."

"Travis, honestly, this is the way I'm most comfortable doing it, okay?"

He would have argued, but she started to keen. The pain on her face was unbearable to him.

When she came through on the other side, she ordered him to pile up the quilts and cover them with all the towels from the closet.

He did what she asked, doubling the quilts. The pile added a buffer against the hard floor in front of the fireplace.

Travis built it up. "Good?" he asked.

"Yes, that's good." She took his hand in hers. "Travis, you need to get up close and personal with me right now."

"What do you mean?"

"You need to check me out, make sure everything's okay."

"You mean…" He tried to swallow, but came up dry. "You mean check down *there*?"

"Yes."

He'd never looked at a woman down there in any way but sexually. "I'm not a doctor. How will I know if anything's wrong?"

"You won't. Or maybe you will. I don't know. I just need you to look."

"Is there any way around it?"

"None."

His harsh breathing filled the room, but he helped Rachel to lie down. She bent her knees, and he lifted up her dress.

Her underpants were damp and stained pink from her accident in the hallway. Correction, not an accident, but a natural part of childbirth.

"I can't take my undies off. Can you do it for me?"

Before he could respond, she let out a groan that seemed to come from the depths of her soul. She gritted her teeth and arched her back.

When she finished, she was panting. "They're coming closer."

"That seemed like a bad one."

"Yeah. They'll get worse."

Worse?

"I don't know what to do."

"That's okay." She arched with pain again. She panted, "My body docs. The birthing will take its course."

"What if something goes wrong?" He was scared shitless. He knew nothing about this. He was a capable guy and wasn't used to feeling useless.

"Everything will be fine. Things feel fine."

This torture was fine?

He wiped her forehead where sweat dripped in what seemed like an unending torrent.

Sure, this was a natural occurrence that had been happening since the dawn of time, but did women have to suffer so damn much?

During the next contraction, with Rachel's back bowed and her hips off the floor, he managed to get her underpants down to her knees. While she relaxed to rest and wait for the next one, he hauled them off.

He checked, even though he didn't know what he was looking for. Not seeing any obvious problems, he focused on trying to keep Rachel calm.

He held her hand, tiny in his, but she squeezed until he thought she would break his fingers. As small as it was in his big palm, why weren't her own fingers breaking?

He knelt between Rachel's legs while her body worked to birth her baby. He marveled when the head started to show…and even more when the baby's body turned to allow the shoulders to come through.

Travis was there to catch Beth.

A sense of wonder flooded him. He'd never known anything to feel so good in his life.

In the second it took to ease her from Rachel's body and hold her, he lost his heart.

This little girl had been talking to him before she was born, and now he held her for real. She in her tiny, red newness had a power over him that he'd never imagined.

She was real. Awesome. Amazing.

Travis held the tiny, as-yet-unspoiled creature in his hands and thought, *I could get used to you. I could get used to holding you. I could certainly spoil the daylights out of you. I could love you, almost as much as I love your moth—*

He halted that thought with the veritable screeching of tires. No way would he go there. Not true. Not true at all.

This was a temporary aberration, this business of having a woman and kids in his home.

Even once Sammy, Jason and Colt got here, he'd be moving on.

This house might be the beginning of Sammy's dream, but it wasn't his dream. They were the reason he'd bought it. Without them, he would still be a wandering cowboy looking for the next job and the next bunk.

His priority, his sole purpose in being in this town, was them—not the widow who lived across the road, even if she did give birth to splendid creatures on his living-room floor.

He used one of the towels to wipe Beth clean.

"You're one tough cookie, Rachel."

"No. Just determined to have healthy babies."

"This one's healthy, all right. Her lungs are, at any rate."

"Give her to me, Travis." She raised her arms to him, but she looked tired.

"Are you sure you're strong enough?"

"Travis, you can seriously ask me that after what I just went through? Give me my daughter."

He rested the baby on her chest. "You look all done in."

"I'm exhausted, but I want to get to know my baby. Can you unbutton my top and my bra? I want her skin to skin. It's good for her to get to know her mama."

He did as she asked, revealing breasts that were heavy and blue-veined. He'd never seen anything more beautiful in his life than this red, wizened baby on her mother's pregnancy-ravaged, perfect body.

Rachel reached her hand to him. He took it. She squeezed, though not as hard as when she was giving birth, thank God.

"Thank you, Travis. I was terrified."

"You didn't seem it."

"I was. I've never been happier than when you came out of your house to get me so I wouldn't have to do this alone."

"I was scared, too."

"I know, but you rose to the occasion."

"I didn't do anything. You did all the work."

She chuckled. "Yeah, I did, didn't I?"

"Thank you, Rachel. This was a gift. Something special. I'll never forget tonight."

He touched Beth's hand. She curled tiny, perfect fingers around his thumb, or tried to. His fingers were huge and clumsy compared to hers.

"Imagine," he said. "Five minutes ago, she didn't exist. It's a wonder."

"Yep. The best wonder on earth."

"What about that?" He pointed to the umbilical extending from her body and still attached to the baby.

"The afterbirth will come out in a minute." She winced. "Soon, I think."

He swallowed hard. "Is it going to be bad? Please tell me you don't have to go through that again."

She closed her eyes, briefly, then said, "No, it won't be that bad. It'll be sort of like aftershocks following an earthquake."

"So we survived the earthquake. Now, your body finishes up for you."

"Yes. You'll have to cut the cord. Wash some scissors in that water you put on to boil, okay?"

"The water!" He raced to the kitchen to find it full of steam. Fortunately, the pot he'd put on was huge and had been filled to the brim. It was still half full.

He dropped his scissors into it and retrieved tongs from a drawer to fish them back out of the boiling water.

Back in the living room, he crouched beside Rachel.

"You have any string?" she asked, her exhaustion clear in her reed-thin voice.

"Should I boil it?"

"No."

He got it from a drawer in the kitchen. By the time he returned to Rachel, the afterbirth lay on the towels between her legs.

He'd seen plenty of farm animals being born and had a rough idea of what needed to be done now. He used the string and scissors to sever the connection between mother and daughter.

He put it into a garbage bag beside the back door. He'd deal with it in the morning. He wasn't going out in this snowstorm.

The howling wind still rattled the old house.

After helping Rachel tidy herself as much as possible, he built the fire back up.

"You warm enough?" he asked into the silence of the room.

She didn't answer. He glanced at her. In the few moments that his back had been turned, she'd fallen asleep. He pulled the quilt up more securely over the baby and the sleeping woman's shoulders.

He stood to pick the two of them up to carry them to his bed when the lights went out.

"Damn. Power outage." In truth, given the severity of

the wind, he was surprised it hadn't happened earlier. He lit the kerosene lamps he had ready and waiting on the mantel.

He nudged Rachel's shoulder. "We need to get you off these wet towels and quilts," he whispered.

The whiskey highlights in her eyes that fascinated him were dimmed by fatigue, but her spirit flashed. "Why?"

"Because the power just went out, and it's too cold to put you in my bedroom. I need to make up a bunk for you down here."

Her gaze flitted around the room. "Tori?"

"I'll take care of her, no worries. First, I'll get the bedding from my room."

He dragged the king-size duvet from his bed along with his pillows.

Back downstairs, he said, "Hang on to Beth."

He lifted both of them onto the sofa, then checked out the state of the blankets that had been underneath her. The towels were drenched along with the top two quilts. The bottom quilt could be salvaged.

He left it where it was and spread his duvet on top of it a couple of feet from the fire.

"Hold on tight." Picking them back up, he put them onto the side of the duvet closest to the fireplace and folded the other half over them.

Getting his sheepskin from the hallway, he covered them with it.

"Travis, we'll die of heat."

"If the power stays out, it will be frigid in here by morning. I'm going to get Tori."

He put the child onto the armchair he'd moved close to the fire earlier. Ghost followed and curled next to her again. He covered her with the duvet from one of the twin beds. She slept through the whole thing.

He lay down fully clothed on the sofa with the duvet from the other single bed and settled in for the night, the only sounds the popping of logs in the fire and the howling of the wind around the old house.

The house had felt empty since he'd moved in. Tonight it was full of loved ones and joy.

Travis had never been happier.

Throughout the night, Travis got up several times to stoke the fire and add logs.

He'd never had more precious cargo to protect.

In the morning, through bleary eyes, he noted that the storm seemed to have abated outside.

A thin wail tore at his heart.

"Rachel," he whispered. "What does she need? To be fed?"

"Already working on it, Travis," Rachel whispered back, and he was engulfed by such a powerful wave of intimacy he wanted the moment to last forever.

He'd never, not once in his life, not even through everything he'd shared with Samantha, felt this close to another person.

He saw her hands move beneath the quilt and then the baby quieted.

In the armchair, Tori still slept, curled up like a kitten under her duvet.

Peace, and a profound sense of happiness, washed through Travis. He loved these girls.

He got up and stoked the fire. Just about to return to his bed on the sofa, he stopped. *Whoa. Go back to that last thought.*

I love these girls.

He returned to his bed on the sofa, laying down with the stunning realization that here in Rodeo, Montana, was a treasure worth more than anything in the world.

He'd traveled all over the western states and up into Canada, not knowing that all the while he'd been searching for this. For them.

You sure? Maybe it was Beth's birth, Read. Maybe this is only leftover emotion from last night's drama.

He searched his heart. His soul. The feeling was deep. True. Since he'd arrived in Rodeo, he'd been steadily falling in love with Rachel.

He'd found paradise and perfection here in Rodeo. But how did Rachel feel about him?

He fell asleep pondering that all-important question.

An hour later, he awoke again to hear Tori stirring.

"Mommy? Where are you?" she asked with a hint of uncertainty in her voice.

She sat up in the chair and rubbed her eyes.

"Easy, Tori," he said gently. "You're okay. You came to my house last night. Remember?"

She nodded. "I'm cold."

Travis stood to stoke the fire yet again. He'd be doing this particular chore for the rest of the day. He doubted crews would get out too early this morning to get fallen wires repaired and power restored.

Rachel shifted gingerly. She poked her head out of her blankets.

"Good morning." She sounded sleepy and happy, if a tad weary.

"How're you doing?"

She peeked under the blanket. "We're good. I should get Tori and me home, though."

His expression flattened. Last thing he wanted was for them to leave. Ever. "Why? What's over there that you need?"

She took a moment to respond and then said, "Absolutely nothing." She looked at her two girls and then at him. She smiled sweetly. "I guess the power's off over there, too?"

"I would imagine."

"I'm still cold, Travis," Tori piped up.

"Take this." Rachel tried to haul the sheepskin off herself. "I'm hot."

"Okay. Here, Tori." He covered her with part of the coat. It dwarfed her. She giggled.

"If we're going to visit for a while, we'll have to put together a makeshift bassinet for Beth."

Tori perked up. "Beth? She's here? Where?"

"Right here," Rachel murmured. "Come on down and meet your baby sister."

Tori crawled out from beneath the coat and tiptoed over.

"It's okay. She's already awake."

Tori knelt on the floor and shivered. Travis crouched behind her to lend his warmth. Besides, he wanted another glimpse of the precious creature he'd delivered last night.

Rachel peeled back the duvet gently. Beth lay against her mother's breast.

Tori wrinkled her nose. "She's little. Can she play with me?"

Rachel laughed. "Not yet. She has to grow a bit first."

Beth's unfocused gaze took in her surroundings.

"She doesn't look awake, Mommy. Can she see me?"

"Not too clearly, Tori. She was only born a few hours ago."

The miracle of the experience still humbled Travis. It flat-out boggled his mind that he'd been part of that messy, spectacular event last night.

Tori knelt to kiss Beth's forehead. Travis steadied her so she wouldn't fall on the baby.

"She's soft, Mommy." Tori patted Beth's forehead.

"Gentle, Tori, like we taught you with Ghost."

The cat, still ensconced on the armchair, lifted her head. She jumped to the ground and ambled into the kitchen where she set up her morning, god-awful yowling.

In his arms, Tori startled. "What's she want, Travis?"

"Breakfast."

"Me, too."

"Sure thing, missy. I'll get right on it just so long as you don't start any of that caterwauling yourself."

Tori giggled.

Travis stood, picked her up and deposited her under the covers and sheepskin on the armchair. "Curl up there and stay warm while I figure out what we'll have. We don't have any power for cooking, but I've got some ideas that might work."

He prodded the log in the fireplace, and the fire flared. "You ever been camping, Tori?"

"What's camping?"

"I'll take that as a no. We're going to have us some camping fun. We'll get to it in a minute. First things first, though."

He stared down at Rachel and the baby. "How do I set up a bassinet? I don't have anything like that."

"Can we use one of your dresser drawers?"

"You can use anything you think might work. I'll go get one."

She called after him. "Bring whatever spare linens and blankets you might have."

"Sure thing," he said from halfway up the stairs he was taking two at a time.

The upstairs sure was frigid. Keeping the first floor warm would be a full-time job today. Good thing he'd prepared for the storm.

He dumped the contents out of one of his drawers and filled it with the sheets from the boys' beds.

Back downstairs he dragged the afghan from the sofa.

"Let's put her over here." Setting the drawer by the end of the sofa nearest the fire, he doubled over the bed sheets innumerable times and used them to cover the pillow that fit into the bottom perfectly.

He crouched beside Rachel. "Hand her over."

With great care, he set the baby onto the sheets. She

let out a tiny squawk before Travis covered her with the folded afghan.

Behind him, Rachel stood. Travis spun around. "Should you be standing?"

"I'm good." She peeked at Beth. "Hold on. I'll set her up properly. Let's get rid of the pillow and put the folded afghan on the bottom."

Travis helped her.

"I need my suitcase," she said.

He retrieved it for her. She took out a couple of small pink blankets and wrapped the baby in them snugly. She took out another blanket, knitted and thicker than the first two, and doubled it up, laying it on top of her.

"We'll have to watch her to make sure she stays warm enough. She's too young for pillows and afghans."

Travis didn't have a clue what she was talking about, but he'd watch her 24/7 if that's what it took to keep Beth safe.

Rachel glanced around. "Um…where's the…um…washroom? Did you keep the one off the kitchen?"

"Yep. It's still there. It'll be cold, though. Let's get you and Tory dressed warmly. We can't spend all day under the blankets."

He stared at Rachel. She still looked tired. "Amendment. *You* can stay under the blankets."

Her laugh belied the dark bags under her eyes. Did nothing keep this woman's spirits down?

"How do you do it?" he asked.

"Do what?"

"Laugh. Enjoy life. Keep happy when there is so much going wrong for you."

"Travis, I have my moments. I have times when I feel overwhelmed, but at this moment, I'm the most fortunate woman who ever lived. I have two wonderful, beautiful daughters."

"She means me and Beth, Travis."

"I understood that, Tori." A laugh that started deep inside his soul burst out of him. This woman with her unbeatable optimism brought out the best in him.

Rachel smiled. "I like your laugh, Travis."

Her smile warmed him from head to toe.

"Why don't you and Tori put on as many layers of clothes as you can stand and I'll rustle up breakfast?"

A few minutes later, they passed him in the kitchen on their way to the bathroom. A second later, Tori yelped.

"It's too cold, Mommy. I can't sit on it."

"You have to."

He heard Tori sob. He knocked on the bathroom door. "Can I come in?"

"Yes." Rachel sounded frustrated.

He opened the door. She *looked* frustrated. Tori hopped around and clutched herself. Clearly the kid really had to go.

"Tori, will you go if I hold you over the toilet without touching the seat?"

"But I haves to take down my pants to go."

"I know. I won't look. See that painting of the colorful fishes?"

She nodded while she hopped.

"I'll stare at that, okay?" He put his hands under her armpits and lifted. Rachel pulled down her pants and underwear, and Travis positioned her over the seat with her little butt hovering without touching. He held her there until her tinkling finished, all while staring at the abstract painting of fish left by the former resident.

He stood her on the floor and Rachel pulled up her pants.

"Better?" he asked.

"Thank you, Travis. Better."

He glanced at Rachel. "You going to need help, too?"

"I'll manage." He heard laughter in her voice. "It's going to be uncomfortable."

"That's putting it mildly. Come on, Tori. Let's give your mom privacy. You can help me with breakfast."

He closed the door behind him and Tori. In the kitchen he was just getting bacon out of the fridge when he heard a much bigger yelp than Tori's tiny one.

"Oh my Lord, it's like ice!" Even from a distance and behind a closed door, her voice carried.

Travis couldn't help but laugh, but also thanked his lucky stars he could do his business standing up.

He carried Tori and the bacon into the living room.

"Tori, do you want me to try to make hot chocolate in the fireplace?"

Her jaw dropped open. "You gots hot chocolate?"

"Yep. I felt bad I didn't have any when you were here decorating for Christmas. I went out and bought some for your next visit."

"That's today! Today is my next visit!"

"Right, but we have no power, so we're going to try to make it using the fire."

He snuggled her into the armchair under her blankets. "Stay put. I need to get a few things from the basement."

Snagging one of the lanterns, he hurried downstairs where he rummaged in a big old box of his camping equipment and came up with a kettle and a small pot. He also found a metal stand he used on campfires.

Back upstairs, he retrieved milk from the fridge and the tin of hot chocolate from the cupboard. He filled the kettle with water.

In the living room, he found Rachel already ensconced on the sofa beside her brand-spanking-new daughter.

"Can you drink normal coffee now? I don't have decaf."

"I don't honestly feel like coffee. May I just have hot water?"

"Sounds kind of dull."

"It will be warm. That's all I want right now. What can I do to help?"

On his haunches in front of the fireplace, he swiveled to look at her. "That walk to the bathroom didn't do you any good. You're pale."

"I just need a little more sleep. It was a long night."

"Yeah, it was at that." He smiled. "And much of it was spent working. If you need to go to the washroom again, I'll carry you."

"That isn't necessary." She craned her neck to look around him. "What are you doing?"

"This is my camping trivet. I'm putting a pot of milk on for Tori's hot chocolate. It'll scald quickly, though. I'll have to watch it."

He went to the pantry off the kitchen and returned with fondue forks. "Your neighbor's British relatives left a lot of interesting old stuff in the house."

"What are those?" Tori asked.

"Fondue forks."

"What's fondue?"

After he explained about fondue, he opened the bacon and wrapped a slice around the fork. When he held it over the flame the fire spit and hissed from dripping fat.

Once the slice was cooked, charred in some parts, he put the slice onto a plate and handed it to Tori.

"Mommy first!"

"Okay. Here you go, my lady, on your Lady Someone-or-Other china."

"Lady Carlisle. Thank you." She blew on it then bit into it. "Oh, that's so good. Why is it that everything tastes better cooked over an open fire?"

"Don't know, but it's true."

He handed Tori her cup of chocolate, but not before topping it up with a quarter cup of cold milk. "Should be cool enough for you, sprout."

"What's a sprout?"

"You ask a lot of questions, kid. Hold that with two hands."

"Travis, could I change my order from hot water to hot milk?"

"Sure."

"No, wait. Save the milk for Tori."

"This is instant chocolate. It can be made with water, too. You need the milk right now more than she does."

"True. Besides there's milk at home in the fridge. Since I won't be there opening and closing the door, it should stay fine for quite a while."

Travis took the chocolate from Tori. "Travis, I'm not finished."

"I know, but I'll hold it while you eat this bacon."

He handed her a strip of cooked bacon on a small saucer. She chewed it and licked her fingers. "That's yummy! Can I have more?"

"Tori, Travis has to eat, too," Rachel admonished.

"She can have as much as she wants. I've got more in the fridge and the freezer. I stocked up."

Rachel stared out of the front window where snow settled in huge drifts everywhere, and where the roads were still impassable.

He handed Tori another slice of bacon.

"What about your sister? Have you heard from her?"

"No. I can't get through to her on her phone. Texts aren't making it through. I'm worried, Rachel."

He felt a touch on his shoulder. Rachel had stood to comfort him.

"I told you to stay seated," he said gruffly, because the worry about Sammy and the boys coupled with last night's experience and now Rachel's proximity left him shaken and emotional.

"Sure." She returned to the sofa and got her plate. "More, please." She looked saucy and not the least repentant for disobeying him, but he understood what she was doing. She was trying to make him feel better, and he was grateful.

He dropped another slice of bacon onto her plate. The next slice went to Tori. Only then did he eat.

"You have a bunch of forks," Rachel said. "Why don't you put on more than one slice at a time?"

Travis shrugged. "We have nowhere to go and nothing to do. Without electricity, it's going to be a long day. There's no sense in rushing."

"True."

The baby started her pitiful thin little cry, and Rachel picked her up. "She needs a change."

She moved to get her suitcase, but Travis stopped her. "What do you need?"

"A diaper and a wiping cloth."

He brought them to her, and she changed the baby while Tori watched. "What's that?"

"That's where her belly button will be."

"Mine doesn't look like that."

"No. Hers will look like yours eventually."

"What are you doing now?"

"She's hungry. I'm going to feed her."

"Does she want bacon?"

"No. She can't eat people food yet. Only breast milk."

"I got milk in my hot chocolate. You can give her some."

"That's just for big girls like you. Beth needs to stick with breast milk for now."

Behind him, Travis heard a long drawn out "ooooh" and peeked over his shoulder. Rachel had the little one to her breast, trying to get her to latch on. He spun about so he wouldn't invade her privacy.

"She drinks from *there*?" Tori said.

"Yes, my breasts are full of milk."

"Mommy, that's silly. You aren't a cow." Tori sounded stern.

"All kinds of creatures produce milk to feed their babies, including humans."

"Does Travis have milk, too?"

He choked on the slice of bacon he'd just put into his mouth.

"No," Rachel answered. "Men don't get milk. Only women do. I have it because I gave birth to Beth."

"Does she like it?"

"Yes. Very much. You used to like it, too."

"No, Mommy, I liked hot chocolate."

"Eventually. Before that, you ate just like this."

"I don't think so." Travis heard rustling and peeked over his shoulder. Rachel lay on her side facing away from him with the baby lying on the sofa, he presumed drinking from the other breast.

He couldn't see anything, so he didn't think he was invading her privacy as he helped Tori get snuggled back under her covers again. When she sat down, a cat's indignant meow sounded.

Tori and Travis both laughed. Ghost had snuck in under the blankets and Tori had sat on her.

He made room for both of them. "I'm going to make toast. Those few slices of bacon weren't enough food for any of us."

"Toast! Yes, please."

"What do you like on yours? Just butter? Peanut butter? Jam?"

"Melted butter."

"Melted butter? Does she mean just normal buttering?" He directed the question to Rachel who spoke over her shoulder.

"Yes."

He stuck a fork through the first slice and held it over the fire. Unfortunately, one side got burned. He scraped off the charred bits, but Tori looked down her nose at it.

"Travis, it's burned."

"I'll eat it while I drink my warm milk." Rachel put the baby back down in her drawer bed and covered herself up again.

"What do you take? PB? Jam?"

"Usually marmalade, but I can live with jam."

"You don't have to. Hang tight." He fetched an unopened jar from a cupboard in the kitchen, buttered the burned toast and spread it with marmalade.

After handing it to her on her plate, he made a less burned one for Tory.

Only then, again after making sure the two of them had enough, did Travis make toast for himself, plowing through a half-dozen slices of bread.

"Do you have a griddle in your camping stuff?" Rachel asked.

"I have one in the kitchen. Why?"

"For lunch we should try making crumpets on the fire." She sounded drowsy. "Do you think we'll still be here at lunchtime?"

"Oh, yeah. No doubt at all."

No response.

He glanced over. Rachel was out like a light.

Travis tucked her in.

He found Tori nodding off with a chocolate mustache. He tucked her in, too.

After building up the fire again, he snagged his sheepskin, put it over himself and sat in front of the fire with his back against the end of the sofa.

How could all of this mundane, unexciting stuff leave him so happy?

Peace, love, happiness flooded all of the cavernous spaces that had lived in Travis since his empty childhood.

Chapter Twelve

Travis hadn't known it, but he'd searched his entire life for this. For her. For Rachel.

All of the miles he'd traveled, all of the ranches he'd lived on, every cross he'd had to bear were all worth it, because all had led here, to Rachel.

He hadn't known he'd been searching. He'd thought the emptiness that dogged him was just a part of life.

After years of being tied down with Sammy, he'd wanted nothing more than to avoid anything that hinted of responsibility. It was enough to keep himself fed, clothed and earn a living.

But take on others? No way.

As much as he'd loved Samantha from the day she was born, he'd also felt responsible for her. His parents had done the barest minimum. Everything else had fallen to him.

He would never tell her so, but there'd been moments, especially as a teenager who couldn't play sports or date or hang out with friends, when he'd bitterly resented his role as mother, father and caregiver.

He'd never known a carefree childhood or adolescence.

How carefree is your life now, Read? Sure, you can go anywhere at any time, but what is it worth?

There was no pleasure in living year after year in bunkhouse after bunkhouse with a bunch of men, many of them strangers for the first few months, and then never seeing them again after he left.

His life had become normal ordinary survival, and that was it.

Where was the joy?

He'd been on the chilly outside looking in at warm places that had never been open to him.

Here, in this living room with a woman and two children who completed him, he was finally home.

Rachel was magic, fantasy, desire and fulfilled longing all rolled into one. The joy she'd given him on the carousel ride on his first day in town was a small taste compared to this entire feast.

They belonged together.

The realization stunned him.

So how did he go about wooing her?

He'd never wanted to stay with a woman permanently before. With Vivian, he hadn't realized until too late that he hadn't been in control. She'd been pulling his strings throughout their relationship.

Even when he'd thought she was the one, he'd held back from making the final commitment, his intuition kicking in on some level. Or maybe he'd just had cold feet.

He felt none of that now. Not one iota. All he felt was a desire to move ahead, to act on feelings he'd never experienced before.

Rachel was a mother with two young children. She'd just given birth. How on earth did he make his feelings known to her?

He couldn't touch her, couldn't offer her his body. Man, after what she'd just been through, those thoughts were the furthest thing from his mind.

Her body would need time to heal. So what did he have to offer her instead?

He didn't know who to talk to or where to go for advice. Who could he ask?

The obvious answer was Sammy, but he couldn't get hold of her.

That thought sobered him and brought him back to earth and out of his amazing euphoria.

"What are you thinking?" Rachel's whisper came out of nowhere.

She was watching him, her face dark that far from the light of the fireplace. He couldn't make out her expression.

"Are you warm enough?"

She laughed. "You have so many covers piled on top of me I can barely move. Shivering isn't possible."

He smiled. "Good."

"What were you thinking about so seriously? What's worrying you? Do you need us to leave?"

"God, no! Why would you think that?"

"This is a lot of responsibility for a single man. You're used to having your space to yourself. Now we're here crowding you."

"Rachel, honey, do you know how many times I wanted to invite you over? I've spent too many years alone. There's more space in this house than any one man could possibly use."

She raised her eyebrows when he called her *honey*.

"Okay, you might have wanted the company of a woman." She didn't say *me*, just *a woman*. As though any woman would do. She didn't get it yet. How could she? He'd never even hinted to her that he wanted her. Travis held in a secret smile. She would understand soon enough. He'd make sure she did.

"You didn't count on having two children here," she continued. "Especially not a newborn baby."

"True. I gotta be honest, Rachel. I like it."

"But this isn't reality. Reality is months of sleepless nights and diaper changes and pureed green peas."

"I've shoveled a mountain's worth of shit in my lifetime. That little thing's diapers won't faze me."

She made a scoffing sound. "You won't believe what this tiny body will be able to produce. We'll see."

"No, *you'll* see." He was dead serious. Only in hindsight, now, did he see that he'd had a connection to Rachel since the first moment he'd seen her on that carousel.

Not just an attraction, but also a deep connection, as though he'd recognized parts of himself in her. And parts of her in him.

His life, his former burdens, and the sight of her pregnant belly had held him back, along with his own fear, but today he saw everything clearly.

He might think it was the high emotion of Beth's arrival, but that was only the catalyst. He could finally see what had been happening from the moment he'd arrived in this town.

Rachel had been on his mind ever since. No amount of resistance had been strong enough to stop the train that had barreled down on him.

Somewhere along the way, he'd decided her family could also be his. *She* could be his family. He wanted that more than anything he'd ever wanted in his life.

"What do you mean, I'll see? What will I see?" A puzzled frown furrowed her brow. "What are you saying, Travis?"

Was it too soon to admit his intentions? He thought so. Best to let things develop more slowly.

The farthest he would go at the moment was, "Will you bring the children over for Christmas? Spend the day with me, okay?"

She didn't answer right away.

"Please?" he said.

Again she hesitated. "What about your sister and her children?"

"You'll like each other. I want you to meet them." *I want Sammy to get to know you.*

"The children would have someone to play with. The boys would like that. So would Tori, I bet."

"Okay. We'll come over. I'd like that."

So would he.

MANY TIMES THAT DAY, Travis paced in front of the window. Snow had drifted too high for him to drive out and get a doctor for Rachel, or to drive her to the hospital. And with the phones not working properly, he couldn't even call a clinic for advice.

She said she was fine, but even so, he worried. He wanted both her and the babe checked out.

The power stayed out for another fourteen hours.

He kept them with him until the following morning, walking them back across to their trailer, carrying the baby while Rachel rested her hand on his arm.

He'd insisted. Sure, giving birth was natural, and she was capable of taking care of herself, but cripes, it had only been a little over twenty-four hours.

He didn't know if there was ice under the snow.

The bottom line was that he didn't want to see anything happen to her. She'd become as precious to him as anyone had ever been.

"I'll bring the suitcase over once we get you settled in," he said.

"I appreciate all of this, Travis."

Tori whooped and giggled in the snow.

"It's a winter wonderland, isn't it?" Rachel said.

"Do you like winter?"

"I like all seasons, Travis. Each one has its good points."

Her optimism, that ability to rise above everything that

went wrong in her life, was what he found most attractive about her.

She found some good in everything. Even when she got really low, she didn't whine, just got on with business.

The trailer felt too empty to him. He didn't want to leave her here.

He'd asked her to stay with him longer, but she'd said, "I need to get on with the rest of my life. No time like right now to do that."

Just inside the front door, she hesitated. He thought maybe she was having second thoughts about coming back. Noting the moment she stiffened her spine and moved forward, he shook his head.

Stubborn didn't begin to describe Rachel McGuire.

Fine. This situation wouldn't last forever.

Rachel didn't know it yet, but her days in this tin can were numbered.

He perched Beth in her cradle in the corner of the living room.

"Still a bit cold in here. It hasn't warmed up fully yet."

"She's well swaddled and cozy. If it's too chilly, I can put her in the carrier and wear her. She'll be fine."

He didn't bother asking what all of that meant, just straightened and looked down at her. "You'll call if you need anything?"

Her skin looked good. Her hazel eyes were clear. The time at his house, getting sleep and doing nothing more than feeding her baby, had done her good.

The bags of exhaustion under her eyes were gone. He wished he could banish them forever.

"Yes, I'll call."

"Promise?"

"I promise. Travis, thank you for everything. I couldn't have done it without you."

"You're about the most capable woman I've ever met,

Rachel. You would have been fine." He tucked her hair behind her ear. He wasn't sure, but he thought he detected a fine tremor running through her at his touch.

Good sign.

"I'm glad you didn't have to do it alone."

"Me, too."

Travis couldn't keep himself from giving in to an urge that had been building for weeks.

He leaned forward and kissed her. He liked the feel of her full lips under his and the scent of his soap on her skin and the breathy sigh that escaped her.

"Travis, you're kissing Mommy."

He pulled away slowly, that one freckle on Rachel's lower lip tantalizing at this close range, tempting him to return for seconds.

"I sure am, Tori." He smiled down at her. "Get used to it."

Rachel's eyes widened.

Travis grinned and left the trailer, whistling all the way across the road to his home.

Inside, it felt empty, though. He wanted them back here now. He didn't want them to ever leave again.

He would make a good home here, one that would put his childhood to shame.

Between him and Sammy, they could sort out where and how everyone would live.

He hadn't understood that there was no burden in love.

When he held Beth, her small weight represented responsibility. He couldn't imagine the commitment it would take to raise her to adulthood, but that responsibility would also come with tremendous reward.

Was she a burden? Never. Would she be a challenge? Yes. Was he up to it? His answer was a hands down, flat-out, resounding yes.

The same with Tori. Even when she was tired and fractious, all he felt for her was affection.

He'd always loved his sister. He loved his nephews more than anything, but the worry of keeping them safe had overwhelmed him at times.

The difference between the two families was that, even though Sammy and her children loved him, he'd lived on the outside looking in.

He remembered thinking that all he would ever know of family life would be to live it vicariously through Sammy and his nephews.

Here, with Rachel and Tori and Beth, was hope and inclusion and possibility and love.

Especially love.

He was a capable guy. He was up for the challenge.

Somehow, he could blend the two families and make it work.

He would fight tooth and nail to make it work.

He set about putting away quilts and washing dishes and planning his campaign to win Rachel McGuire's heart.

After the snowplows came through, he drove into town and stopped in at Cole's office.

"Rachel McGuire had her baby." Travis explained what had been happening. "I need to get a doctor out to see her. Who should I talk to?"

Cole gave him a name and an address.

"He's probably her doctor. I kinda doubt Rachel was seeing anyone else. Doc Chambers does everything around here."

Travis stopped in, introduced himself and told him about Rachel. "Can I ask you to go out there to pay her a visit, make sure she and the baby are healthy? I'd compensate you up front."

"I've heard from Rachel. I'm heading out there in an hour to check on her."

"I'd still like to be the one paying for this visit." He

paid and then drove home, more settled now that he knew she'd be taken care of.

Sure, it was a high-handed decision, but doctors and hospitals were expensive, and he knew he had a heck of a lot more money than Rachel did.

This way she wouldn't have to dip into any savings she might have. She could use her money for the next few months until she could get back to work.

The second his phone worked again, he called Samantha. She answered on the second ring. Hallelujah.

"Where've you been?" He sounded angry, but cripes, he'd been worried.

"What do you mean? I'm in San Francisco. Where else would I be? We didn't plan to leave for a couple of weeks."

"I've been calling and calling and not getting through."

"Really? My phone's been on. I've been here. Did you try texting me?"

"I did everything but turn myself inside out."

"I don't know what's wrong, Travis. Maybe there's something wrong with the phone. It has been acting strangely, but I didn't know calls weren't coming through. I'll get it checked out."

"Do that. We had a storm here, but I was calling you before the weather rolled in."

"What's wrong? What's got you so upset?"

He told her about Vivian.

"That she-snake," she said. "No offense, Travis, but I never did trust her."

"Now I understand why."

"I don't think it matters what Vivian said about Manny and his men."

"How can you say that?"

"I got a letter from him. From Manny."

"He's not supposed to know where you are!" Fear settled in his belly, messing with the lunch he'd eaten a while ago.

"He doesn't. Apparently it went to his defense attorney and then to the prosecutor who sent it along to me."

"What did he want?" Talk about a snake who shouldn't be trusted.

"It was a weird letter, Travis, but…"

"But what?"

"I believe everything he wrote in it."

"Like what?"

"He's found religion. He's turning over a new leaf."

"Come *on*, Samantha. *Seriously*?"

"I worked for him for two years. Plenty of long hours. Lots of overtime. I got to know him well. This sounds different."

"All of a sudden he's a new man?"

"He said he's called off his boys. They're no longer looking for me."

"So within the space of a couple of weeks, he gets Viv to tell him where I am, where you plan to live and then turns around and calls off his goons?"

"It was a long letter. He said he gave Vivian a bunch of money to set herself up in an honest business. He gave his men what he had left. He said he won't need it anymore."

"And you believed him?"

"Every word."

Travis scratched his head. "Aren't you being naive?"

"No, I don't think so, Travis. He's old. He has no family left. I think prison changed him."

"I'll believe it when I see it. In the meantime, when are you and the boys leaving?"

She hesitated then said, "Do you mind if we come in February instead of for Christmas?"

Thank God for Rachel and the girls coming over for Christmas, or he'd be feeling hollowed out right now. "Why?"

"Remember how upset Jason was about the trial and moving so much and about his dad leaving?"

"Yeah."

"Well, he's joined the drama club at school and loves it. They're putting on a musical before Christmas and a play at the end of January. He really wants to do them."

Travis reined in the hurt that had started up in him, that his nephews didn't want to see him as much as he wanted to see them. It made sense for Jason to find something for himself.

"This has stabilized him, Travis. It's given him some peace. I'm going to uproot him again to bring him to Montana, so let him have these two experiences first."

Travis didn't respond, even though he understood.

"Okay, Travis?" Samantha asked.

Finally, he answered, "Yeah, okay," and it was. Whatever was best for Jason was fine by him.

"Sammy, one more thing…"

"What?"

"There's this woman…a really nice one…she has two children, girls, and I, well…" He didn't know what Sammy would think. "I guess I've kind of fallen in love."

"It's about *time*, bro." Samantha laughed and hooted. "What's she like?" She didn't sound disapproving. Just curious.

"The best person I've ever met."

The tension in Travis's shoulders eased. Sammy approved. She would like Rachel. "I don't know how we'll work out the living arrangements."

"Relax, Travis. We'll make things work. Can't wait to meet her."

A week before Christmas, Travis drove into town.

He hadn't seen any movement at Rachel's, no comings

and goings, and it hit him. How was she getting out to get groceries when she had a newborn?

He'd heard through the grapevine that Cindy had not just left the trailer, but she'd actually skipped town.

If he went across the road and offered to pick up groceries, he had no doubt Rachel would say they were all fine.

Instead, he planned to just show up with food, but he had to be crafty about it. He'd tell her he was inviting himself for dinner…and it was a potluck and he was bringing the food.

Clever, Travis.

After the storm, he'd been called to the ranch to help with snow clearance and winter chores. He'd put in long days.

At night, he shoveled her driveway so she could get out if she needed to.

She might have had visitors. He was gone so much during the day he couldn't know for sure.

This foray into town to pick up groceries for her was really an excuse to go see her.

He picked up ready-made stuff. From the grocery store's small deli counter, he picked up a cooked rotisserie chicken along with a box of potato wedges.

In the meat department, he stared down entire shelves of steaks. If he picked up a couple for her and Tori, she would see it as charity.

It wasn't. It was love.

He didn't have experience in this new, fledgling love business, but his instincts told him it was too early to tell her how he felt.

Right, then. Subterfuge, it is.

He would just have to tell her he didn't want chicken. He wanted steak.

He chose four filet mignons.

Lastly, he got a bag of ready-made salad and paid for it all.

Next stop…Vy's diner.

"Hey," he called when he walked in. "Those look good. Are they spoken for?"

Vy stood behind the counter, frosting a batch of cupcakes. She looked up and smiled. "Nope. I just felt like baking."

"Can I buy half a dozen to take out?"

Vy's dark brows rose to the kerchief she wore when she worked around food.

"You having a party?" She turned up a cup and poured him some coffee.

He shrugged. "Sort of. I guess." He sat down and sipped the hot brew. "I'm taking a bunch of food over to Rachel."

"Isn't that baby the cutest little thing you've ever seen?"

"When did you see her?"

"I stopped in three days ago."

"Do you know if she's had other visitors?"

"Sure, the other girls came with me. We brought new baby clothes. Some really cute stuff. People have been in every day making sure she's okay."

"I didn't know. I've been busy at the Double U. I haven't been over."

"I heard you delivered Beth."

"Nah. She delivered herself with her mother's help. I was just there to catch her."

She covered his hand where it rested on the counter. For a fraction of a second, he wondered if she was making a pass. It wasn't ego. It had just happened too many times in the past.

She cleared up that misconception when she said, "Thank you. Rachel means the world to us. We're all grateful you were there for her."

Briskly, she wiped down the counter and got out a box in which to package his cupcakes.

He listed everything he'd picked up at the grocery store to take to Rachel's and added, "I wonder if maybe she'd like some soup."

"Great idea. Whatever you all don't finish tonight, she can reheat for lunch tomorrow." She bustled into the kitchen and returned with two canning jars of soup, which she put into a big paper bag. "You can return the jars the next time you come in. I have a hearty minestrone and a lovely parsnip soup."

Travis made a face. "Parsnip?"

"Don't knock it till you've tried it. Parsnips, cream, a little fresh ginger, and a texture like silk on your tongue."

"I'll have to take your word for it."

"Try it. That's an order. You'll be back here tomorrow for more."

"Won't promise that much, but I will give it a taste." He pulled his wallet out of his back pocket. "You know that great meat loaf you make?"

"You want some of that, too?"

"Give me enough for the girls for tomorrow night's dinner."

Vy raised one perfectly shaped black eyebrow. "The girls?"

Travis blushed. "Rachel and Tori."

"They wouldn't by any chance be *your* girls, would they?"

Travis sobered. He was full to bursting with love for them, but didn't know what to do with it other than confessing it all to Rachel and hoping for the best.

Gossip could rage through a small town like a forest fire, but Travis had a good feeling about Vy. He'd eaten in here often enough to get a handle on her. Something about the protective way she talked about Rachel inspired a trust he didn't show a lot of people.

"You gotta promise you won't tell anyone, not even those women helping with the fair. I do think of them as my girls. I love Rachel."

Vy had been leaning one hand on the counter and one on her hip, in her usual cocky pose, but now her mouth fell open and she straightened to her full height. "I was joking. I didn't know... Oooooh."

She covered her head with her hands. "I think I'm going to explode. I've wanted Rachel to be happy for so long. Davey was a great guy, but... Rachel needs someone dependable."

"I know it seems fast, but—"

"No," Vy interrupted. "It is *not* too fast. It's about time someone recognized Rachel for the gem she is."

She leaned across the counter, grasped the lapels of his coat and hauled him toward her. She had a good grip. She laid a smackeroo on first one cheek and then the other.

"Thank you." She wiped moisture from beneath her eyes without smudging her perfect makeup, a skill that awed Travis. "I can't think of a better man for Rachel."

Hard-headed Violet was a softie. She swiped her thumbs across his cheeks to get rid of her lipstick, he guessed.

"Have you told her how you feel?"

"Not yet."

"Give her time and space. You'll know when it's the right moment."

She went into the kitchen and returned with another container, placing it in the bag on top of the meat loaf.

"These are all warm, so I'm putting the cupcake box into a separate bag. Keep them apart so the icing won't melt."

He paid for the food and made to leave, but she stopped him.

"I'm giving you something extra for Rachel from me." From a cold display case, she took out large bowls of rice pudding and custard. Spooning them into two plastic containers, she said, "Tell Rachel she needs the calcium in these. They're both loaded with cream and milk."

He thanked her and left, breathing out a sigh. He hadn't realized until now just how nervous he'd been about the town's reaction to a newcomer, a relative stranger, laying claim to one of its loveliest women.

Vy's approval warmed him through and through.

Now to see if Rachel would accept all of this food.

Instead of turning into his own driveway, he drove into hers.

He took the bags from the diner and carried them to the door. While he waited for her to answer, a crowd of nerves took to line dancing in his stomach.

The door opened. Rachel looked surprised to see him. He drank in the sight of her. She looked tired, but not that beat-down exhaustion he'd seen while she'd been working in the bar.

Her hair was mussed, and she looked both womanly and sleepy. What would she do if he slipped his arms around her and held her?

Man, he yearned. He wanted all of the things that had been missing all of his life, and he wanted them now. This moment.

She yawned.

Covering her mouth, she said, "Sorry, you caught me napping."

Damn. He hadn't thought about that. "Sorry! You want me to come back later?"

Tori squeezed between the door and her mother's legs. "Travis! What's in the bags?"

Direct as always. He laughed. He'd missed her. He glanced back at Rachel. He'd *really* missed *her*.

A gust of wind kicked up, and Rachel shivered. "Come in out of the cold."

And didn't that sum up his entire life? He'd been on the outside looking in for too long time.

He stepped into her trailer. It might as well have been the grandest home in town. He was happy to stand and stare at Rachel all day.

Again, Tori piped up, "But, Travis, you didn't say what's in the bags?"

He walked to the minuscule table they ate their meals on and set the bags down.

"First, I have to ask your mother something before I open the bags."

Tori hopped from foot to foot, staring at the bags he knew she recognized from Vy's place.

"Ask her quick, Travis."

He crossed his fingers with a smile and said, "Rachel, I know this is sudden, but I'm hoping you don't have plans. Can I stay for dinner?"

"Yes!" That was Tori. Her fingers rested on the edge of the table, clearly itching to open the bags. "Say yes, Mommy."

Smiling ruefully, Rachel answered, "I can't very well say no, can I?"

She was right. She couldn't disappoint her daughter.

Yep, craftiness paid off.

He opened the bag with the meat loaf and jars of soup. Next, he took out the rice pudding and the custard. "These two are from Vy. She says you need the calcium."

"That's so sweet of her."

"What's in that bag?" Tori asked, pointing to the one he hadn't opened.

He knew from his nephews not to bring out dessert until dinner was finished. "That's for later. Let's put it in the kitchen."

"Travis, this is so nice of you. It's kind of early, but I wouldn't mind digging in right away, if you don't mind."

"Sure, but there's more."

Her voice took on the hard edge he recognized as her streak of independence. "More?"

He pointed to the food on the table. "Rachel, how far do you think soup's going to take me?"

After a swift glance down his body, she said, "Okay."

"I have a favor to ask before I get the rest of the food from the truck."

"What do you need?"

"Can you dress the little one to play outside? You can eat the calcium-filled food while we play for a while. Okay?"

"You're a gem. She's been going stir-crazy with me."

"Good. It's cold out. Dress her warmly."

He retrieved the rest of the bags from his truck and came back. Rachel gaped.

"Now, don't get your dander up," he warned. "Once I decided I was coming for dinner, I got excited and picked up some of my favorite foods."

He unloaded the bags onto her kitchen counter.

"Can you put the hot food into the oven? Tori and I are going to grill some steaks."

"On the barbecue? Outside?" Rachel peered through the window. "It's freezing out there."

"Yep. We won't be long. Tori won't get cold."

"I'm not cold! I'm hot!" The child stood like an over-stuffed beach ball in her winter coat and scarf and big mittens and hat.

"Let's go." He picked up the steaks and left before Rachel could complain that he'd bought too much food.

Across the road at his house, he made Tori stand inside the front door while he got his grilling implements, spices and a clean plate from the kitchen.

Outside, Tori started rolling a couple of large snowballs to build a snowman while he pulled the grill out of the garage and turned it on. He seasoned the steaks and threw them on once it had heated up.

"Travis, this is heavy." Tori struggled to put one ball on top of the other. She'd made them too big to handle all by herself. He helped her, but realized he didn't have anything to use to dress it.

He did the next best thing. He picked up the child and tossed her into a pile of snow he'd created when he'd cleared his driveway.

She shrieked. Her laughter floated on the air and filled his heart.

"Again!" She scrambled off the top and launched herself into his arms. He caught her and tossed her back up to the top.

This, *this*, was joy, and fun, affection and love. Playing in the snow. Grilling food for the girls he loved.

He flipped the steaks and continued to toss Tori around in the snow. The kid really had been stir-crazy. She had a lot of energy to expend.

When the meat was cooked, he put it on a plate, switched off the barbecue and walked back across the road with Tori.

Inside the trailer, Rachel had effected a stunning transformation.

The small table was covered with a lacy cloth and only one lamp burned. The effect was more cozy than romantic. Good thing. This was a family gathering.

He would get to the romance later.

Or maybe this was part of it.

Was romance only about flowers and wine, expensive dinners and lovemaking?

Couldn't it also be about showing love in the smallest ways? In easing burdens and sharing responsibilities? In consideration and cooperation and just plain everyday affection?

He hoped so, because he had a lot of these simple things to give to Rachel and her girls.

There were only two folding chairs at the table. That's all that would fit.

Rachel leaned over a bassinet on the tiny sofa. "Beth has been asleep for a while, but she should go a little longer."

She picked up Tori's small plush armchair.

"I'll have Tori eat in her own little chair."

"Uh-uh, Mommy. Want to eat with you and Travis."

"But there's no room."

"She can eat on my lap."

Rachel looked hopeful. "Are you sure?"

"Yep. We'll make it work, won't we, Tori?"

"Yep. We make it work."

The food lined the counters in the kitchen. Travis added the steaks to the spread.

"Let's dig in," he said. "I'm starving." He picked up Tori and settled her onto his arm and took a plate in his other hand.

"What do you want? A little bit of everything?"

"French fries!"

"That's all?"

"Yep."

"Nope. You'll eat meat and salad, too."

"'Kay."

Beside him, Rachel hummed low. It sounded like a laugh lurked in there somewhere.

"Funny," she murmured. "She never agrees with me that easily."

"Must be my charm."

The sassiness he'd encountered on his first morning in town shone through in her laugh. "No doubt."

He liked sharing jokes with her.

While he held a plate, Rachel filled it with a bit of

everything, except soup. He wasn't a soup kind of guy. He'd bought it for her.

He sat on a chair with the little one comfortable in his lap.

Rachel placed a small mug on the table beside his plate.

"What's that?" he asked.

"Parsnip soup."

"Um. I'd rather not."

"Vy said you'd say that. She said you made a face when she mentioned parsnips."

Surprised, he asked, "You talked to her?"

"She phoned and said—and I quote—'Make sure macho man tastes the soup.'"

He took umbrage. "Macho man?"

"I think she was joking. You've made a conquest there."

"Why would you say that?"

"Vy's not easily won over. She can have a really hard edge. When she talks about you, though, I can hear affection in her voice, especially when she called you macho man."

Travis stopped chewing. Was that—? Did he hear *jealousy* in Rachel's voice? Did she think there was something going on between him and Vy?

That could screw up everything he wanted to build.

In a rush to set her straight, he opened his mouth, but pulled up short. Nah. This felt good, too good to end so early.

Rachel McGuire had feelings for him, no doubt about it. Oh, yeah, she sure did.

She liked him. She really, really liked him.

He cut bits of chicken and steak into pieces for Tori then dug into his own meal, feeling at peace with the world, in the finest state of contentment he'd ever known.

He tasted the soup. Vy was right. It was excellent. Smooth as silk, just as she'd said. He'd have to tell her that next time he visited the diner.

They ate in silence for a while until Rachel asked, in a

tone he knew was meant to be nonchalant, "Is there anything you want to share?"

"Share?" he asked, playing ignorant.

"About you and Vy?"

While he might be enjoying Rachel's jealousy, he didn't want her to be unhappy.

He set down his fork and laid his hand over hers. Startled, she glanced up at him. In her gold-flecked eyes, he saw both defiance and hope.

"I'm here. With you. With your girls. I'm here because I want to be." He turned her hand over and placed a kiss on her palm. "I'm here because I want to be with you."

She stared at him and licked her bottom lip.

He leaned forward to kiss that tiny freckle, but Tori put her little hand up to his face.

"Here! Kiss my hand, too, Travis."

Ha! The joys and complications of having children around.

Throughout the rest of the meal, he watched Rachel. She looked flustered, but happy and that made him happy. Her cheeks were red. A good sign?

The baby fussed, and Rachel left the table to sit in an old armchair to feed her.

"Did you have enough to eat? I could bring your plate over to you."

"I'm so full, Travis. That was a lot of food." She sent him a shrewd glance. "I'm on to your tricks, you know. This is far, far too much food for one dinner."

He grinned, unrepentant. "I know, and before you say it, no, I'm not taking any of it home. It's for you and Tori."

"Thank you." She said it quietly, and he knew it hurt her pride, but he also heard relief.

"You had enough, Tori?"

She nodded and he set her on the floor. She ran to a box in the corner, pulled out some Legos and started building.

"I'll put the leftovers away. Where do you keep your plastic containers?"

She told him, and he packaged up the leftover chicken, steak, salad and soups.

When he opened the refrigerator door to put it all away, he got a shock. There was next to nothing in there other than a few condiments and a carton of milk. What would she have done for dinner if he hadn't come by?

He damned Cindy to hell and back for leaving her daughter in this situation. Just when Rachel needed her mother the most, the woman was gone.

Cindy should have been here buying groceries, or baby-sitting so Rachel could get out.

"I'll get you some more groceries when this stuff runs out. You need more milk for Tori for tomorrow?"

"Just milk, Travis. Nothing else. No, wait, a loaf of bread, as well. Can you get my wallet? I'll give you money for it."

"I'm not taking mon—"

"Travis, please." Her jaw jutted as she dug in for a fight.

There came a time when you just had to allow a person her pride. He carried her purse to her. She took out her wallet and handed him a five-dollar bill.

He managed to get a quick peek inside. It was all she had. So the problem wasn't just not being able to get out to get food. It was also not having money, unless she had oodles in the bank.

Somehow, he doubted that.

Otherwise, there would be more in the cupboard than peanut butter.

Anger raced through him, but he held it in check.

What Rachel and her children needed most right now was not high emotion, but simple acts of support and kindness.

If he ever saw Cindy again, though, he'd tear a strip off her hide.

"Anyone want a hot drink with dessert?"

"Dessert!" Tori abandoned the Legos and wrapped her arms around his legs. She did that a lot.

The spontaneous act filled him with wonder.

He could get used to being part of a family.

That sign of jealousy in Rachel could be a start. He knew she found him attractive. He knew she liked him.

Could she ever love him?

He made tea for Rachel and hot chocolate for Tori and put out the box of cupcakes with small plates from the cupboard.

They sat in the living room because Rachel still held Beth, who had finished her dinner at her mother's breast.

Tori made it only halfway through her cupcake before lying down with her head in Travis's lap and falling asleep. All that playing in the snow had worn her out.

After he'd finished his dessert, Rachel said, "Beth is sleeping. Would you like to hold her?"

"Yeah."

Her brows shot up. "I'm surprised. I thought infants would intimidate you."

"I held my nephews a lot when they were little. Their father was AWOL most of the time."

Rachel brought the baby to him and snugged her into the crook of his arm.

"Did your brother-in-law travel for business, or something?"

"Yeah. Something. He was always running off to different ashrams and yoga retreats and meditation conferences."

Rachel covered Tori with a blanket. "Sounds like a man who is trying to find himself."

"That's all fine and dandy, but he should have done it before having kids. Once you've made that commitment, those kids are more important than anything else. Kids don't ask to be born."

"True."

Of course she would understand. Her own father had run off and left her behind.

Silence settled over the trailer.

Tori slept soundly, as did the baby in his arms.

Again that sense of peace that this small family brought with it came over him.

In time, he gave Beth back to Rachel and carried Tori to bed, tucking her in fully clothed.

At the front door, Travis pulled on his boots and coat.

"Thank you, Travis. You gave us a real gift today. It was wonderful to have more than just our own company."

She pointed one stern finger his way. "But don't do it again. I can take care of myself and my children."

"Yes, ma'am." He leaned forward, kissed her gently on her lips and smiled.

Just before stepping out of the trailer, he said, "See you on Christmas Eve."

"What? I thought we were coming on Christmas Day."

"You are. Sammy and the boys aren't coming until February. They won't be here for Christmas. I want to have you all over for supper on Christmas Eve, too."

When she didn't respond, he leaned in. Her eyes dropped to his lips. Obviously, she thought he meant to kiss her again.

She didn't step away, and in fact, seemed to move closer.

So, she liked him *and* she desired him. Perfect.

"You have any plans for Christmas Eve?"

She shook her head.

"Good. Bring the kids over at five."

He left his truck where it was and walked across the road. After cleaning the barbecue and putting it away in the garage, he closed the front door with a big smile on his face.

Chapter Thirteen

Rachel bundled up the children and drove into town.

She needed to get the last of her money out of the bank.

What she would do after Christmas when it was all gone was still a question. She wondered if she could get an advance from Honey.

But then what would she do when she was working and not getting paid because she'd already borrowed it and spent it?

Her stomach roiled. Her mind balked at applying for welfare or any kind of public assistance. Grimly, she thought, *I will if I have to.* It would take a while to come through. What would she do in the meantime?

In town, she parked and got Tori out of the car, then Beth.

In the bank, she talked to Ethel, the aging teller who'd been there all of Rachel's life.

"Can I withdraw a hundred, Ethel?" That would leave another forty to last through Christmas.

Dear Lord.

For now, she needed a hundred to get more groceries, oatmeal, powdered milk and more diapers for Beth. She was just about out of the supply she'd put by before giving birth.

Ethel frowned. "Didn't you know, Rachel?"

"Know what?"

"Oh, dear, I'd hoped it was okay. I'd hoped she'd asked first."

Dread weighing on her shoulders, Rachel didn't need to ask who *she* was. Cindy. Rachel had put her onto the account after Davey's death, for when she gave birth and Cindy would have to buy food for Tori.

Obviously a foolish move, but she'd thought she could trust her own mother.

"What is it, Ethel?"

"Cindy cleaned out the account before she left town."

Rachel locked her knees to keep herself upright. She breathed through her nose so she wouldn't get light-headed.

"I see. Okay, thank you, Ethel."

She left the bank quickly, with her dignity intact.

She would get through this. She would survive.

Dear God, how?

IN THE DAYS after their meal together, Travis hadn't made the mistake of taking more food across the road. He'd known Rachel wouldn't accept more even if he invited himself to dinner.

In another few days, he'd be feeding them all on both Christmas Eve and Christmas Day.

Sitting in the diner one morning, he perked up when he recognized Rachel's car pull up and park across the street.

She got both children out of the car and went into the bank. A short while later, she came back outside. She didn't look happy.

"Vy, come here," he called.

When she did, he said, "Sit down." She slid into the window booth across from him and followed the direction of Travis's intent stare.

"What do you want?" she asked.

He pointed. "Does she look happy to you?"

Rachel finished strapping both of her children into the

car. She rounded the hood and got into the driver's seat, sitting there without starting the engine.

There was no missing the deep unhappiness on her face.

"No," Vy said, and Travis glanced at her. Her mouth drooped in a grimace. "What's going on, Travis?"

"I think Rachel's out of money."

"Impossible. She's worked hard at Honey's. She had to have been saving to get ready for this time. She has a good head on her shoulders."

"I would have thought so, too." He explained about the empty refrigerator and cupboards. "I caught a look at her wallet. She had nothing."

"Look." Vy grasped his arm. "She's driving back out of town without stopping at the grocery store. Would your groceries have lasted this long?"

"Nope. We have to do something." He corrected himself. "*You* have to do something. She won't take any more from me, but if her friends stopped in, each a few days apart, with supplies, she might accept that."

"That's only temporary. What about after Christmas?"

"Vy, I hope to God I will have convinced her to change her living situation permanently by then."

A broad smile split her face. "Yeah?"

"Yeah." He threw forty bucks onto the table. "That's to cover my sandwich and some food for Rachel. Can all of you work out a schedule between you?"

He stood and retrieved his hat. Before leaving he said, "Leave Christmas Eve and Christmas Day open for me. I'll be taking care of things then."

"You got it, Travis." She took off her apron.

"Will!" she hollered to her cook. "I need to go to the pharmacy for diapers and wipes. Oh, Lord, what else would she need for the baby?"

Travis shrugged. He knew stuff about babies only second hand.

"Don't worry," Vy said. "I'll raid my stores here and bring her eggs, milk, flour. All kinds of stuff."

To Will she hollered again. "Wrap up a bunch of that fried chicken and mashed potatoes and a container of the pasta carbonara to take out. I'll be back in a few minutes to deliver it personally."

CHRISTMAS EVE ARRIVED. To Travis, it seemed to have taken forever to get here.

He fussed with the food, more nervous than he could ever remember being. He had a lot riding on tonight's dinner.

The evening started at five o'clock in deference to the two children. They arrived on time.

At the door, Travis took Beth so Rachel could take off her coat. She hung it with Tori's beside his. Travis liked the look of their coats hanging together.

He wanted to see them there from now on.

"Travis, look. Mommy curled my hair."

"She did a good job. It's beautiful." He noticed that Rachel had taken care with her own appearance, as well. Her hair was full and curly. From the first moment he'd set eyes on Rachel, he'd wanted to run his fingers through her hair. That urge was even stronger now.

In the living room, he noticed something else. She'd lost much of the weight she'd had when she was pregnant. He'd never seen her normal figure before, and he liked what he saw. A lot.

"I'll take Beth and undress her." When Rachel took the baby from him, the side of her breast brushed his forearm, and his desire for her shot through the roof.

Quit it, Travis. This is a family night.

He had to get this relationship settled before his un-requited lust sent him 'round the bend.

Not only that, he just plain wanted these girls in his life forever.

"Where's that drawer we used for Beth before? Can we use it again?"

"You bet. I emptied it earlier just in case." He brought it to the living room, and Rachel put the baby into it. They covered her with the receiving blankets Rachel had brought over with her.

"She's cute as a button, Rachel." It was no lie. The child was beautiful.

"Me, too. I'm cute as a button, too, aren't I, Travis?" Tori tugged on his pant leg.

From his nephews, Travis knew all about sibling rivalry.

He picked up Tori and twirled her around. "You bet! You're the cutest button in the jar."

She giggled while he twirled her until they were both dizzy.

Dinner was beef stroganoff and crusty bread. Vegetables weren't his thing, but he'd included steamed green beans.

They ate in the dining room on the Lady Carlisle plates that Rachel loved so much.

They had one of Uma's homemade apple pies for dessert only because she'd put Travis to work peeling a mountain of apples. She'd made ten pies for Christmas and had given him one to take home.

After apple pie with vanilla ice cream, they sat in the living room. Tori sipped hot chocolate while the adults drank decaf coffee.

Deep satisfaction filled Travis.

The evening ended too soon.

"Travis, can you come over in the morning to see what Santa left for me?" Tori asked at the door.

He'd be honored. Life with these girls brought joy on top of joy on top of joy. "Sure thing, sprout."

She slammed herself against his legs and yelled, "You're my best friend."

With a quiet smile, Rachel left with Beth in her arms. They made their slow way across the road and the snow-covered ground in front of the trailer bathed in the cool winter glow of a full moon.

Only after they'd made it inside their front door did Travis close his door.

The following morning, he awoke early as excited as any kid on Christmas morning.

He dressed with care and walked across the road in the darkness. They were in for a few months of dark mornings. Some of the ranch hands minded, but Travis didn't. He liked mornings. The sun hadn't yet crested the horizon. His breath frosted in the early-morning air. He knocked on the door.

No answer.

He knocked again.

Finally, the door opened and Rachel stood in an old plaid robe belted at her waist. Her rumpled hair begged to have his fingers untangle it. He wanted to bury his face in it.

"Am I too early? I thought Tori would be up by now."

She started to laugh, couldn't seem to stop, and he stared, bewildered.

"Rachel, what is it? What's wrong with you?"

She wrapped her arms across her waist and kept laughing. He frowned and got exasperated.

"If you don't tell me what's so funny, I'm leaving."

Laughing too hard to say anything, she threw her arms around his neck so he wouldn't leave.

He hadn't bothered to button his coat for the short walk across the road, so her full breasts flattened against the white shirt he'd put on. Only a couple of layers of fabric separated them.

He clung to her as though his life depended on it. In a sense, it did.

In his arms, she quieted and stopped laughing.

"Um, Travis, you should let me go."

"Never, Rachel," he whispered fervently. "I've wanted you from the first moment I set eyes on you."

"Impossible. I was more than seven months pregnant." Her breath brushed his ear.

He kissed her neck.

She moaned. "Don't do that, Travis. I'm a mother."

He chuckled. "Mothers don't like to be kissed?"

"Mothers love it." The sentiment seemed to have popped out almost against her will, and Travis chuckled again.

He kissed her neck and ran his tongue along her jawline.

She pushed against his chest and stepped away, straightening her hair self-consciously.

"We can't do this."

"Yes, we can. I care for you, Rachel. I have since the day of the carousel ride. Hell, I'll admit it. I love you."

She stared with a deer-in-the-headlights shock. "You can't."

"I do."

When she didn't respond, he tucked her hair behind her ear. "Do you have any feelings for me in return?"

"It doesn't matter what I feel. I come with two kids, Travis."

"I'm aware of that, Rachel. So?"

"So…we're a complete package. You can't have me without them."

"I'm aware of that, too, Rachel. I love those two little girls already."

"This isn't possible. Stuff like this doesn't happen. Men don't fall in love with pregnant women and take on ready-made families."

"This one did and will."

"Okay, that's what you think now, but what about next

year? You don't stay anywhere, Travis. You travel around. I can't do that."

"I'm not doing that anymore, either. You give me more than I thought was possible. Joy. Happiness. Stability. An end to loneliness. Did I say joy?"

They stared at each other, a showdown of wills, Rachel still unbelieving.

She looked away first. "I need coffee. Make us a pot while I get dressed."

"Why were you laughing at me?" He knew he sounded hurt, but what on earth had been Rachel's problem when she'd answered the door?

From halfway to her bedroom, she started to laugh again.

"It's five-thirty in the morning, Travis."

Feeling like a damned fool, a hyperactive little boy in a man's body, he cursed himself for not checking the time before he'd left home.

His cheeks heated.

Midway through making the coffee, he started to laugh, too.

Christmas Day turned out to be the most perfect day he'd ever lived.

Dinner was perfect, and both Tori and Rachel loved the presents he'd picked out for them—a pretty mauve sweater for Rachel and a tiny pink cowboy hat for Tori. He could imagine it hanging on a hook at the diner with all the adult hats.

He hadn't expected anything in return, but Rachel had knitted him a black scarf. He would make a point of wearing it often.

The only fly in the ointment was that she refused to talk any more about his loving her. Worse, she refused to admit that she cared for him in return.

He walked them back home, Tori with her pink cowboy

hat perched on top of her winter hat, but Rachel scooted inside before he could kiss her good-night.

He had no idea what was holding her back.

Did he have to *prove* his love somehow? Okay, sure, he would do anything, but *what*?

WHEN TRAVIS VISITED the following afternoon with containers of leftovers, Rachel didn't know what to think, or what to do.

She already knew she loved him, and he claimed to love her, but she'd chosen the wrong man before.

Davey had been fun, enthusiastic and as likable as all hell, but he hadn't been dependable.

Travis seemed dependable, but had a history of moving every five minutes. How on earth could she trust that he would stay put?

Thank goodness the children were napping because he got down to business right away.

"What's holding you back?"

She'd already broached the subject of his nomadic lifestyle yesterday, so she told him what else bothered her. "Since this is a serious topic, I'll be honest, but this is hard for me to talk about."

Travis leaned forward and rested his elbows on his knees. "What can be that bad? You're strong, honest, attractive...just about perfect."

Although touched by his flattery, she resisted it. "When Davey and I started dating, he told me he'd also been interested in another woman, but chose me instead. I knew the woman. She was pretty. Gorgeous, actually. After Tori was born, I asked him why he chose me over her, and he said it was because so many other men were attracted to her that he could never be sure she wouldn't be tempted by someone else."

She stared out the window. "I, on the other hand, he had

complete faith in. I was, in his words, like a worn-in pair of cowboy boots, always ready and waiting by the front door."

A laugh burst out of Travis, and Rachel frowned. "What's so funny?"

At her combative tone, he sobered. "The man was a fool. Yes, you are steadfast and loyal, but I don't want you in my life for that. Not solely for that. I want you physically. A lot. I want your affection. I want to be treated with love and respect the same way you treat those kids of yours. And I want to give you that in return."

He knelt on the floor in front of her.

"When I look at you, I see the woman I want in my life for always." He grasped her face in his hands and kissed her, not a head-spinning, gymnastic-type of kiss, but a slow and deep and earnest promise.

He pulled away and she stared into his deep blue eyes. This couldn't really be happening. Travis Read loved her.

"Rachel, you are so damned attractive. Did growing up with your vain mother leave you feeling plain? You aren't. I was attracted to you from the first second I set eyes on you."

He stood and put on his coat. "Just as soon as it's possible to leave Beth for a couple of hours, I'm taking you out on a date."

"But—"

He left without waiting for an answer.

Rachel brushed her fingers across her lips, because that promise in his kiss had been tempting and so, so sweet.

To dream about possibilities or not to dream? That was the big question for a woman who'd been burned by dreams in the past.

Travis called Vy and arranged for her to babysit Tori and Beth for a couple of hours in two weeks. He'd done an internet search to find out when it was okay for a woman to be able to make love after giving birth, and that seemed to be the earliest.

He couldn't think of another way to convince Rachel of his love than to show her with his body.

She wasn't believing his words.

He went straight to Rachel after he hung up and told her in no uncertain terms that they were going to have a date and that Vy would take care of the children.

He knew the women had continued to drop off food and supplies periodically since Christmas. He didn't know what Rachel thought of that.

That Saturday night, mid-January, rolled in cold and clear.

Rachel drove off, presumably to take the children to town. She came back soon afterward and parked in his driveway.

He opened the door and watched her walk up to his steps and up onto his veranda, remembering the times she had waddled here. He'd found her attractive then, but this version of Rachel knocked his socks off.

She stepped into his house and did something unexpected.

Without warning, she grasped fistfuls of his shirt and dragged her to him, kissing him as though only tonight existed, as though there were no tomorrow.

He didn't resist, but fell into it with all of his heart.

"No dinner, Travis. Let's go upstairs now."

"Rachel." She wouldn't let him look at her. He forced her to step back. "What's going on in that head of yours? Why the rush?"

She wouldn't meet his eye.

"Are you—" He tilted her chin up with his hand. "Rachel, are you nervous?"

She nodded.

"Why?"

"You've known a lot of women. I don't have a lot of experience. There was a brief friendship with a guy in high school and then only Davey after that."

"What does experience have to do with anything? It's about feeling good with each other. I love you. Do you feel anything for me besides desire?"

She nodded, but didn't say anything. How much did she feel, he desperately wanted to know.

"Are you sure you want to go upstairs before dinner?"

"Yes. I really do. Travis, it's been so long, and I've wanted you since I saw you that first day."

He smiled, wonder coloring the moment. "You have?"

"Yes. I'd really like to get over being so nervous. I won't be able to eat a thing."

He took her hand and led her upstairs to his bedroom where he lit one candle. "That okay?"

He kissed her gently, soothing more than arousing. She seemed to like it so he kept it up.

In time, she melted against him.

He unbuttoned her blouse and slipped his hand inside.

Her breasts were full, ripe. He slipped her blouse from her shoulders and reached around her to unhook her bra. In his wildest dreams, he never imagined they would be awkward with each other.

He let his desire guide him.

He took one nipple into his mouth, keeping his touch gentle. A quiet moan slid up her throat.

"Is that okay?"

"Yes," she whispered. "Travis, I've wanted to see you for so long. Let me."

She undid his shirt and slid it off his shoulders. "Oh, Travis, I do like your shape. So much."

"And I like your body. Let's undress and get into bed."

"First, Travis, wait. I have to do this." She undressed fully and stood in front of him. She looked nervous.

He drank in the sight of her. She had a pretty body, with a tummy still soft and full from having carried a baby. Lines crossed it horizontally. No wonder. That skin had done a lot stretching.

"You hate my stomach, don't you?"

"What? No." He finally figured out what was worrying her. "Did you think I was looking for perfection? Rachel, this body has nurtured two beautiful girls. Why do you think that can't be attractive?"

The worry fell from her like a dark cloak gliding to the ground.

"Couples expect that their partner's body will change over the years, but this is the first time you're seeing me, Travis, and it's right after I've had a baby."

"Rachel? Do me a favor?"

"Anything."

"Get into bed so I can love the daylights out of you."

She smiled and scrambled into bed.

He undressed while she watched him. Once under the covers, they reached for each other.

He took his time arousing her, first because he was nervous about hurting her so soon after the birth. Secondly, he wanted to soothe her nerves.

She, in turn, seemed to want to please him, reaching for him while he was reaching for her.

They got in each other's way.

Rachel threw herself onto her back and laughed. "We're trying too hard, aren't we?"

Travis rose above her and grinned, leaning on one elbow so he could watch her reaction while he touched her.

He circled her nipple with one finger. "Yeah. I want to make you happy."

Her breath hitched. "Oh, you do, Travis. You make me so happy. I want to make you happy, too."

"So, let's go with the flow. Let's take as long as we need to, and make each other happy." He replaced his finger with his lips.

"You're right. Oh!" She made a cute little noise in her throat. "That feels good. This isn't a race. We have a little time." Her words became breathy. "We can take turns loving each other."

"Right. Let's do that."

That sentiment lasted all of two minutes, and they were all over each other again.

He kissed. She licked.

He tasted. She savored.

They got in each other's way again.

"Don't remember this ever being a problem before," Travis murmured while he paid homage to her other breast.

"Me, either."

Self-conscious, Travis set himself the task of losing himself in his senses. Flowers had nothing on the way Rachel smelled. Her skin felt like the softest of flower petals under his fingers as he stroked her everywhere.

Her moan brought him relief. They were going to be okay together.

He entered her and found bliss. Holding himself still above her, he watched for signs of pain but saw none.

He'd never in his life made love to a woman he loved, and it changed everything. Every touch sizzled, every word sparkled, and every high dazzled.

He could do this every night for the rest of his life and never get enough.

Rachel ran her palms over his chest. "Oh, Travis," she breathed. "You are so beautiful."

So was she. Breathtaking. He began to move.

When she came, he sighed. When he came, he roared with pleasure.

RACHEL LAY IN Travis's arms sated and relieved.

Their lovemaking hadn't been sexy or lusty or passionate, but awkward and sweet, and about as satisfying as anything Rachel had ever experienced.

It had been lovemaking on a deeper level than ever.

Intense contentment washed over her, along with thoughts of possibility. Travis couldn't be more earnest if he tried.

She knew deep in her soul that Travis had changed profoundly since his first day in town, that what he was offering her was true and real.

That this might, against all odds, turn out to be permanent filled her with hope. What more could he possibly give her but hope for a secure, happy and loving future?

She laughed, filled with happiness.

"Are you good?" he asked, his voice rumbling in his chest beneath her ear.

"Yes," she whispered. "I'm euphoric. And you?"

"Yeah, that word says it all. I want you in my life forever, okay?"

"Yes. I want that, too. Remember the day you had us over to decorate the tree?"

She felt him nod.

"I knew for certain that day that I loved you."

"You did?" His voice filled with wonder. "I had no idea. We'll work out living arrangements somehow. We have some time until Sammy and the boys arrive."

"What are you saying, Travis? Are you asking me to live here with you?"

"I'm asking you to marry me." He cursed. "I don't know how to be romantic. I should have bought a ring and champagne."

"Travis, you're giving me love. I don't need champagne. I'm drunk on love for you."

His eyes widened and he kissed her deeply.

She told him about Cindy stealing all of her money and anger flashed on his face. "Let's not talk about it now.

There will be no negatives in this bedroom, only love and wonder and happiness."

With long languid strokes, Travis learned the contours of her body.

She caressed his chest, his body strange and new, yet the man achingly familiar already. She wanted him again. And again.

"Sorry that was so awkward." Travis nuzzled her shoulder. "I'm usually more skilled."

She moaned softly. "Travis, if you turn more skill on me, I'm not sure I'll survive, because that was wonderful."

She touched his cheek. "Yes, it was new, but I loved that. That was our first time and it was perfect, in all of its getting-to-know-you glory."

"Nice way to put it." He held her jaw. "Know what I think?"

She stared at his mouth, fascinated by it. "What do you think, Travis?"

"The second time's going to be even better."

She stared wide-eyed for a long time and finally whispered, "I can't wait."

"Know what else?"

"No. What?"

"We don't have to wait."

She reached for him and said fervently, "Thank God."

Vy called a little after ten.

Rachel's children missed her and wanted to come home.

Travis and Rachel hadn't even eaten, but had stayed in bed and had played with each other endlessly, their love being made manifest finally and irrevocably in more than just words, but also in the sweetest, and sometimes hottest, of gestures.

Travis loved how responsive Rachel was, and how inventive.

He didn't question how all of this was possible. He just thanked his lucky stars he'd found this town and Rachel. The joy she'd given him that first day on the carousel, that stunningly simple gift, was nothing compared to the universe of honest, unbridled feelings she bestowed on him now.

The lost wandering cowboy had found his home.

Travis drove into town with Rachel to pick up the children, sated and thrilled and filled with giddy delight. Rachel was well and truly his future. "Rachel, why didn't Vy just come out to the trailer to babysit? Everything would have been easier."

Rachel squirmed. "I can't share Vy's history, or her confidences, but she only comes to the trailer when she has to and doesn't stay long. She…um…has a problem with trailers."

Despite the curiosity raging through him, Travis said, "Fair enough. The woman has a right to her privacy."

When they arrived, Vy looked upset.

"I don't know what I'm doing wrong," she said. "I can't get Beth to settle."

The second Rachel took the baby into her arms, she stopped her pitiful crying and closed her eyes.

"I think it was too soon for me to leave her."

"I guess," Vy said, but Travis heard the doubt. She glanced at him while Rachel urged Tori into her outdoor clothes.

"And you, Travis?" Vy whispered. "Was your night better than mine?"

He leaned close. "Vy, it was the best night of my life. Know what else?"

"No, what?" she asked.

"I expect every night after this one will get better and better."

"I'm glad. For both of you." Her soft smile might look sad around the edges, but he didn't doubt her sincerity.

"Come on," he said to Rachel, "I need to take my family home."

They stepped outside of Vy's apartment and approached the car. "We're your family?" Tori asked.

"Yep. You're my family now. What do you think of that?" He held his breath. He had no idea how the child would react.

"Yeah! Are we having a sleepover at your house?"

Travis shot a questioning look at Rachel.

She smiled, all womanly and soft around the edges. Then she laughed and said, "I don't know. Do you think he might serve us bacon cooked in the fireplace again?"

"I'll cook you whatever you want. Anything on this earth."

"Can we sleep in front of the fireplace again?" Tori queried. "I liked it!"

"Sure, sprout." Travis shot Rachel a rueful grin. There'd be no more lovemaking tonight.

"We'll have to get married as quickly as humanly possible," he told Rachel.

"Sooner!" Rachel said, grasping his hand and squeezing.

"Are we going to live with you, Travis?" the pipsqueak asked.

"Yep, from now on and forever and ever. I'm marrying your mom."

Tori clapped her hands. He switched on the radio and Tori started her high-pitched warbling with the music. It would take a lifetime to get tired of this family.

His family.

He thought back over his life and his journey from lonely little boy to burdened adolescent to wandering man to this perfection here in Rodeo, Montana, with his new family.

He imagined days spent turning his land into a ranch and little Tori into a cowgirl. Little Beth could be anything she wanted to be and he would support her. And, oh yeah, he wanted more kids.

That thought led him to the nights he and Rachel would share, and the perfection of the lovemaking they'd shared that evening, and loving the daylights out of her for the rest of their lives.

He couldn't help but smile.

"That's exactly what I like to see on a man's face," Rachel said just before kissing him and making his dreams come true. "A smile."

* * * * *

Come back to RODEO, MONTANA,
to read Sammy's story in RODEO RANCHER
by Mary Sullivan.
Available in March 2017
wherever Harlequin Western Romance
books are sold.

REQUEST YOUR FREE BOOKS!
2 FREE NOVELS PLUS 2 FREE GIFTS!

⊕ HARLEQUIN®

ᴗWestern Romance

ROMANCE THE ALL-AMERICAN WAY!

HWRI6

SPECIAL EXCERPT FROM

♦ HARLEQUIN®
™

ᴅWestern ᴅRomance

*After their spontaneous reunion results in twin babies,
rancher Wyatt Lockhart insists on staying close to
Adelaide Smythe…even if the proximity makes it hard to
remember why he should stay far away…*

Read on for a sneak preview of
THE TEXAS VALENTINE TWINS,
the latest book in Cathy Gillen Thacker's series
TEXAS LEGACIES: THE LOCKHARTS.

"When were you going to tell me?" Wyatt Lockhart
demanded, furious.

Adelaide Smythe looked at the ruggedly handsome
rancher standing on the front stoop of her Laramie, Texas,
cottage, and tried not to react. An impossible task, given
the way her heart sped up and her knees went all wobbly
any time he was within sight.

Ignoring him, she picked up both duffel bags of baby
clothes, blankets and burp cloths, and carried them to her
waiting SUV.

"I wasn't."

Wyatt moved so she had no choice but to look up at
him.

He looked good, but then he always looked good.
Radiating an impressive amount of testosterone and kick-
butt attitude, he stood, brawny arms folded in front of
him, legs braced apart. Backed against the rear corner of
her vehicle.

His gaze drifted over her as if he were appraising one

of the impeccably trained cutting horses that he bred and sold on his ranch. "You didn't think I would find out?"

She lifted her chin defiantly. "I knew your mother might mention it."

Wyatt stepped back. "My mom knows?"

It was her ranch. Of course Lucille Lockhart knew Adelaide and her six-week-old twins were moving temporarily into the Circle H bunkhouse!

Adelaide marched back to the porch. She picked up the large monogrammed designer suitcase that held her own clothing. The one that, unfortunately, had accompanied her on another, fortuitously ill-begotten, trip.

The way Wyatt was eyeing it said he remembered, too.

Ignoring the heat and strength radiating from his tall body, Adelaide stepped around him and headed for the porch. Unable to help the defeated slump of her slender shoulders, she asked, "When are you going to let our last mistake go?"

He joined her on the porch. "I never said making love with you bothered me."

"Then that makes two of us," she drawled, refusing to admit how small his six-foot-three frame made the portico feel.

Wyatt's gaze roamed her postpregnancy frame, dwelling on the voluptuousness of her curves. "Enough to go again?" he taunted softly.

Adelaide stiffened. "Not if we were the last two people on earth," she vowed.

Don't miss
THE TEXAS VALENTINE TWINS
by Cathy Gillen Thacker, available February 2017
wherever Harlequin® Western Romance®
books and ebooks are sold.

www.Harlequin.com

Turn your love of reading into
rewards you'll love with
Harlequin My Rewards

**Join for FREE today at
www.HarlequinMyRewards.com**

Earn **FREE BOOKS** of your choice.

Experience **EXCLUSIVE OFFERS** and contests.

Enjoy **BOOK RECOMMENDATIONS**
selected just for you.

PLUS! Sign up now
and get **500** points
right away!